TEMPORARY PEOPLE

TEMPORARY PEOPLE

a fable

Steven Gillis

Black Lawrence Press
New York

Black Lawrence Press
New York
www.blacklawrencepress.com

Book design: Steven Seighman

ISBN: 0-9768993-6-1

To my mom - the constant voice, forever with love.

You beat the grass and probe the Principle,
Only to see into your nature.
Right now, where is your nature?
                                    - Zen Koan

To pass freely through open doors, it is necessary to
respect the fact that they have solid frames.
- Robert Musil, from *The Man Without Qualities*

All we are saying
is give peace a chance.
                                    - John Lennon

BOOK 1

CHAPTER 1

The babies' heads are fat as fruit grown ripe beyond all natural measure. I remember the first time I saw one, her woebegone look and swollen scale, with hair stretched out in gossamer patches, as ill-proportioned as an artist's lampoon. Startled, I couldn't help but stare and wonder what had happened. Three months later, as the numbers rose and hinted of an epidemic, the truth came out and to no surprise gave us Teddy Lamb, a.k.a. the General.

———

In the center of the Plaza, Teddy has built an enormous movie screen, some forty feet high and ninety feet wide. Night and day clips are shown from Teddy's past performances, footage from *General Admission* and the film he's now making. All Bameritans are included in the current cast, are given roles and costumes, our parts and outfits

STEVEN GILLIS

changing constantly. In the last ten months I've
been dressed as a pirate, a peasant, and a wealthy
industrialist sporting a silver suit and leather
briefcase filled with stones. My acting is poor
and I make no effort to improve. For many years
I've run a small business, selling insurance to my
neighbors, an idea I had following the War of the
Winds and the death of Tamina.

My thinking was simple. Feeling as I did,
as gutted as a road struck deer, I was looking for a
way to recover. The policies I created offered coverage against any sort of injury suffered through
acts of revolution, governmental gamesmanship or
political terror. Teachers and store clerks, day
laborers and farmers arrived one by one to discuss
my plan. I found a reliable partner to invest the
proceeds from premiums as I knew nothing then
and still know little now about handling money.
The funds were pooled, the receipts put into international stocks. I took the profits and expanded
my business, offered group coverage to private
companies, college students and civil servants.
With my success I lived comfortably and placed a
percentage of my earnings back into the community,
helping with schools and charities and such. All
of this was easy, an uncomplicated plan, limited
in sophistication and - because this is Bamerita -
there for others to copy and corrupt.

———

The cameras Teddy uses are state of the art
and mounted throughout the capital for constant
filming. Teddy insists his movie making is for the
good of all, the way he observes us and orders us
about meant, he says, to bring us closer together.

11

As everyone's on tape, collectively and systematically recorded, the implication of his claim is open to interpretation. He tells us his way of creating films will change how motion pictures are viewed forever. He says he plans to submit his film to all the major festivals where he expects to sell distribution rights for millions of dollars. Few of us care. We've had enough of Teddy and his movie business, have tired of his other schemes and offenses. The sentiment is widespread, and still I worry about the consequence of our discontent and where things will likely go from here.

The scenes for Teddy's movie are shot out of sequence and no one can say for certain what the film's about. Even when the soldiers come and order us into our costumes, we're not shown a script. At best, we hear rumors that the movie's a multi-generational saga weaved through the telling and retelling of a 3,000 year old fable. The focus of the fable changes however, each time the rumor's repeated. Teddy reviews all the daily rushes, assesses the caliber of our performance. Everyone's uneasy about how they appear. The perception we give is not always as intended. Our fear isn't artistic but rather a concern for our safety. In evaluating the scenes, Teddy's impatient with people who disappoint him. Those found deficient are removed from the film and rarely heard from again. "That," Teddy says, "is show biz."

———

In Bamerita our history is like the rim of a wheel made to turn around and around, our political cycles nothing if not redundant. Teddy's taking over our government has us less surprised than disappointed and people are restless to overthrow the bastard. We're an old island, ancient by western standards, populated well before Jesus, Tao, the Bhagavad Gita and Dutch Reform. At 4,600 square miles, Bamerita is moderately sized, smaller than the Bahamas though larger than Aruba and Barbados combined. Our population is 1.5 million. We currently sit on a longitudinal line of 36 degrees, 300 miles southeast of the Azores Islands, our waters warmed by the Mediterranean and the Bay of Biscay, some 2,000 miles south of Reykjavik, Iceland.

I say "currently sit," as we're an island unmoored, a body created by enormous volcanic eruptions deep in the ocean sending up pumice and ash, limestone and molasse. Pyroclastic surges have lifted us, much as the islands of Hawaii were formed and continue to be affected by the steady explosion of the Lo'ihi sea mount active for millions of years. A composite of fire and stone fused into ignimbrite - the volcaniclastic rock commonly known as "tuff," where other land masses have settled, their plates idle and magnetic pull of their Curie Points no longer swayed by the steady motion of the waters, Bamerita remains susceptible to shifts in substratum and palaeomagnetic indiscretions. The same forces that lead Gondwana and Atlantis to ride the waves and whole continents to drift apart like pieces of a jigsaw scattered, now float us back and forth upon the tide.

Ethnically, we're a mix of Mamaties, Kalmuns and Dataks. Our religion is Catholic, Muslim and Jewish, our language Spanish, Arabic and English; the latter dominating our shops and schools, newspapers and books. Our first revolution was the War of Redemption in 1305, as then-King Porett XXIV introduced Bamerita to Greek philosophy, Athenian Democracy and the Technology of Allotment. A constitution was drafted, our laws and liberties codified, a parliamentary form of government created with ultimate authority retained by the King. Jai Datisa, the army's Major-General and a parliamentary representative for the northern city of Lobre, opposed the plan to leave so much power vested in the throne. By summer the debate turned violent. Men on horses, with broadswords and claymores, raided villages known to back the King. Before Porett could respond, the revolt swallowed him whole. The King was taken from his palace, bound and weighted with stones and tossed into the sea.

As conqueror, Jai Datisa disbanded parliament and installed himself as Potentate. Since then, the cycle of revolution has continued. Rebellions and coups occur with remarkable frequency, give rise to new governments, intervals of democracy followed by periods of tyranny and further revolt. (Jai Datisa was himself assassinated in 1327, as he relieved his bladder near a eurasian tree, his throat slit by a boy who would be king.) Forty years ago my father fought in the War of the Sorrows, while twenty years later I helped start the War of the Winds. Our success each time seemed promising though wound up shortlived. Recently Teddy Lamb marched thirteen members of then-President Dupala's cabinet down to the water, strapped them to single logs, cut their feet and set them adrift. President Dupala was chained to two logs, the waves pulling his legs left and right until he was split in half and his entrails fed the fury of fish beneath. A month later, the movie-making began.

———

Last week I stood on the scaffolding surrounding the tower I built for Tamina and called to
those who came to speak with me about rebellion.
"I'm sorry, but I can't help you."

Emilo below, kicked at stones, yelled back,
"Sure you can!" He waited until I climbed down,
squeezed my arm, said "Get your dress shoes,
André," and dragged me to a big-headed baby funeral.

"Starch and sugar," Paul Bernarr explained
how the manufacturer of Good Baby replaced
nutritional supplements in milk powder with
cheaper ingredients. "Babies fed the counterfeit
formula are undernourished."

"But their rosy cheeks?"

"A sign of malnutrition."

"So they starve?"

"Eventually, yes." Dr. Bernarr said, "Teddy's
found himself another windfall. The poor are easy
marks."

I paced among the graves. Emilo in black
jeans, brought his guitar. Some folks with no time
to change came in costume, wore medieval outfits,
panne corsets with decorative inserts and flared
peplum bodices, brown slacks and vests. Muske-
teers in large hats and boots and velvet tunics lowered the tiny casket into the ground while Emilo
played, "The River of Babylon," followed by the
Beatles' "Revolution." ("Well you say you want
a rev-uh-loo-tion.") Soldiers appeared and frightened the mourners standing near the grave, got
them to sing a different tune.

We left the cemetery around 5:00 p.m. and
headed back to Emilo's shop. Emilo kept his guitar out while we walked and continued playing. At

the start of the War of the Winds he'd fronted a band called 'Mr. Marker.' The group was named for Chris Marker, the radical documentarian, founder of the French collective SLON - la Societe de Lancement des Oeuvres Nouvelles - whose seminal works included, "Far From Vietnam" and "Be Seeing You." Mr. Marker played a mix of reggae, calypso and American pop, appeared on the local circuit of bars and clubs until the military dragged then-President Kenefie from his office and left him dangling from the roof of the Museum of Natural History. Overnight, the new government censored all artists' work. Unable to play in clubs, Emilo started an underground movement, wrote two new songs - "Junta Heartache" and "The Half Finished Bridge" - which became the anthem for our National Bameritan Democratic Front. Twenty-some years later the NBDF was being resurrected to take on Teddy while my name, along with Emilo's and Justin Avere's, was circulating in places I wish they wouldn't.

Emilo strummed Marvin Gaye's 'Mercy, Mercy Me,' said "Sing it with me, André."

"Ah, things ain't what they used to be."

"That's it."

"War is not the answer."

"What? Whoa. No. Wrong song."

"Picket lines and picket signs."

"That's not 'Mercy,' it's 'What's Going On?'"

"Right."

"But I said 'Mercy.'"

"Mercy me. Don't punish me with brutality."

He stopped his playing, slid his guitar strap around so that the guitar hung behind his back. On the night Teddy staged his coup and dragged President Dupala from his office, Emilo found four large buckets of red dye and a thick bristled brush he used to paint the words, "Koupe tet, bioule kay!" across the rear walls of the Ministry of Interior, Enforcement and Defense. The phrase "Cut off the head, burn down the house!" - was first chanted in 1804 by Jean-Jacques Dessalines, the Haitian slave leader who organized a revolt against the armies of Napoleon. Hoping to inspire a similar response, Emilo waited for others to join him, but the army had a vice grip on the capital. The night passed and the next afternoon the painted words were removed by Teddy's soldiers using sandblasters, ammonia and steel wool.

We crossed Kefuntin Boulevard, the sun hot on my shaved head. After Tamina died, I cut off my hair, fitfully at first, and then routinely as I began to study Satyagraha following the war. I was looking for something to throw myself into, some way of becoming constructively lost, and stumbled onto Satyagraha in a book while drunk. I reread the chapters again the next afternoon, learned what I could about self-help, self-sacrifice and faith without fear. Satyagraha lead me naturally to Ghandi and passive resistance, the movement described as, "An all-sided sword. It never rusts and cannot be stolen." Before Teddy, I thought if I was ever to raise a sword again it would be this one.

A sign above the camera on Forbushe Avenue directed all "non-performers" where to walk. Traffic was rerouted, cars removed from the curbs. A few blocks from Emilo's shop, we stopped in a designated viewing area to watch part of the day's filming. A woman in a brown burlap skirt, a peasant costume complete with grey cloth apron and dung-soled leather shoes, was fighting with three soldiers dressed as livery hands. We stood behind the orange barricades and observed the woman struggle and cry out as the other actors pounced and grabbed and fell on top of her. The violence was not choreographed, was fluid and free flowing, given over to what Teddy called "method acting."

Here again, we could only worry how such a performance fit the arc of the film's overall plot. Our suspicion had long been that Teddy was more interested in blurring the lines of reality than finishing a film, that he was looking for a way to present all acts of violence as make believe, and in so doing, confuse what was and wasn't part of our normal daily life. Those who raised such a claim in public soon found themselves cast in roles that proved life did, in fact, all too closely at times imitate art.

Much of the woman's clothes were torn while the soldiers mounted her in ways that looked entirely real. The cries and groans stirred the crowd. After three or four minutes, a voice through a speaker hidden in one of the jacaranda trees called, "Cut!" We all waited then as the soldiers got up and adjusted their costumes before helping the woman to her feet. A robe was brought and the woman bent forward. There were scratches on her face and arms and bite marks on her neck. The crowd watched as she straightened herself finally and forced a smile. The soldiers, as always, assured us that everything was fine. A few in the crowd applauded on their own, while others did so only as additional soldiers approached the barricades and instructed us to cheer. I recognized the woman then as one of Adim Furle's daughters, and tried to reach her, but the soldiers pushed me back.

"Acting is it?" Emilo took my arm as we walked off. "What we need to do," he said, bending first to stab his penknife into the front tire of a government jeep. I stepped to the side, looked back as Rachel Furle was being helped from the street by a group of peasant women. Emilo swung his guitar across his chest and broke into a loud verse of "Junta Heartache." The first time I heard the song I was a young father, married to Tamina. My own father, Gabriel Mafante, was editor of the Bameritan Sentinel. A supporter of President Kenefie, my father wrote a series of articles condemning the military for its latest coup. In response, the government removed my father as editor and took control of the press. When he continued publishing essays in a private print, the government charged him with sedition and threw him in jail. Emilo, Justin and I organized a series of protests, formed the NBDF, did what we could until we were forced to flee the capital. I moved my mother, Tamina and our children - Anita and Ali - to a safe house and went to join the rebels in the hills.

We were at best a ragtag band of novice revolutionaries, outnumbered and without supplies, forced to scramble for old rifles, boots and food and ammunition. After two months the weather turned wet and then dry again, the breeze off the ocean filling the air with the smell of recent battles. The skin on the soles of my feet peeled away, the colors in the photograph I had of Tamina bleeding from the heat. I lay with her picture between my hands and chest at night, recalling days before the War when we would walk at night to the water's edge, explore the coves with candles lit and our shoes left at the shore.

We remained in the hills another two months. The military government was run by three colonels who directed the War from a position of safety inside the capital. Impatient, convinced they could crush us in one major assault, they ordered their soldiers into the woods the second week of October. We were overwhelmed and in retreat made use of the only advantage we had - our superior knowledge of the hills. The soldiers charged and we laid traps, dug pits and planted spikes covered with twigs. Emilo and Justin placed explosives triggered by wires, while I hid with the others in tall grass, buried by dirt and sod, and opened fire. The soldiers blitzed and we circled around their perimeter, struck and fled, fired and ran. Our strategy allowed us to survive the first wave, and then the second, and still if not for luck we'd have lost the War for sure.

From their bungalow in the capital, having coordinated their army's offensive by radio, the three colonels anticipated an evening of frolic with several young girls, and as an aphrodisiac, downed a large serving of mussels and snails. The meat in the shells had spoiled however. The colonels soon bent and barfing, collapsed in a heap, cramped and shit themselves to death by morning. Without command, the soldiers became splintered and easily picked apart.

How we danced during the Day of Deliverance, a jig for me in Pyrrhic victory. Twenty years later, I shook my head and shouted down at the others from atop my tower, "I can't help you," when they came and asked me to join them against Teddy in yet another war. "What don't you understand?" I pointed at the stars, and the pictures posted on my tower, explained for those too young to remember what happened, how a half mile from

the capital, before I could get home, the last of
the government soldiers with silver daggers and
puffed muscled stabs found Tamina as our children
looked on. "The way," they said, "your baby pups
did wail."

———

In short sleeves, Emilo's right arm showed
a blue tattoo outlining the head of a woman. On
his left arm the letters "A POS" were pricked into
his skin with black ink, the reference to his blood
type, a trick those of us who joined the War of the
Winds borrowed from soldiers of earlier rebellions. We cut across the designated streets, stopping every block so Emilo could attach to building
fronts and the bark of trees those flyers he carried
in his back pocket. The tracts accused Teddy of
profiting from Good Baby. I watched for soldiers,
spotted too late a jeep speeding toward us a block
from Emilo's shop.

The soldiers braked at the corner, pulled
down the last flyer Emilo posted, raced toward us
again and cut us off. The one soldier holding the
flyer was no more than a boy dressed in a worn
brown uniform a size too large. He shoved the flyer
flat against Emilo's chest, asked "How's business?"
laughed and waved as the jeep drove off.

Turning, we saw the soot clouds rising from
around the corner, the smell of smoke reaching us
as Emilo ran and I followed. The smoke from the
fire created a haze which gathered above the pile
of instruments the soldiers had pulled from inside
Emilo's shop and thrown to the curb. Guitars and
basses, reeds and recorders, sound equipment,
pics and bows, banjos and fiddles, all smashed and

doused with gasoline. I jumped with Emilo into the flames, our shoes and pantlegs singed as we stamped about, kicking through the remains for anything worth salvaging.

The entire block was otherwise empty, people having rushed inside their own shops and houses at the first sign of trouble. Emilo cursed and held up the charred neck of a violin, waving it like a wand. We spent the next several hours cleaning up what was left of the shop, sweeping the floor, resetting the shelves, carrying off broken glass and inventory completely ruined. Sometime after 11:00 p.m. we stood outside and drank from a second bottle of anisette. "Sucks, André. You see what happens?" He looked around at the absence of people there on his block and spit into the ash.

I tried changing the subject, mentioned the piles of garbage at the curb. "Tomorrow we need to get rid of the trash."

"You're right. The trash."

"Before it draws rats."

"Rats, exactly," Emilo laughed. "We have too many rats as it is. But we can't get rid of a rat with just cheese, can we? We need the springtrap to crush his skull." He stomped behind the pile of amps and keyboards shattered, and grabbing the back of a broken ukulele, whipped it frisbee-style over my head. "Koupe tet, bioule kay," he made a toast.

I pulled at the front of my shirt to release the heat, went and stood further down the curb where, looking east, I could see the top of my tower in the distance. At forty feet, squared through the base and rounded like a silo, the shadows fell toward the capital each morning and covered my house at night. The outer skin was papier mâché, weather-proofed with lacquer, the frame held together by wires and wood molded deep inside. A week after returning from the War of the Winds, only a day removed from Tamina's funeral, with Anita and Ali asleep and my head a heavy slosh of sour peach brandy, I went into the yard and pasted Tee's picture to a single block of wood. For several minutes I sat in my yard, then walked back into my house and got an article on Dr Subandrio, the one-time foreign minister of Indonesia and chief architect of then President Sukarno's 'guided democracy.' Dr Subandrio had hoped to bring modern reform to the Indonesian archipelago, but was caught in a military takeover and sentenced to death. The penalty was later commuted, though Dr Subandrio remained imprisoned for thirty years. I glued the article on Subandrio beside the photo of Tamina, I don't know why.

Each night now I go back into my yard, cutting and pasting additional photographs and articles to more wood and wire, working with hammer and nails on the base of a tower I never meant to build. Emilo saw me staring off and came to stand next to me. "In the moon, André, no?" He handed me the anisette, waited for me to nod and drink. I appreciated the gesture and told him in turn, "Not to worry, we'll have your store up and running again in no time."

"Sure, sure," he touched his shoe to the trash. The whiskers on his cheeks were dark ink dots, his hair a bushy black with flecks of grey. "You want to do something?" He pointed back down the street, chanted lines from still another revolution. "Cuffee! Cuffee! Cuffee! Rise, Sally, rise! Help me wake them."

"It's late," I got us moving from the street upstairs to Emilo's apartment. His place above the shop was small, filled with instruments and sheet music, old and new recordings on vinyl, tape and CD. Emilo found the guitar he brought to the funeral and sat in his chair where he started playing Bob Marley's, 'I Shot the Sheriff, But I Did Not Shoot the Deputy,' followed by the first chorus from, 'Junta Heartache.' "Oh the devil's at our gate/In a souped up '68/Waiting to see/What will it be/Weak knees or revolution/To halt this Junta Heartache."

Drunk, Emilo's fingers still performed, his voice craggy but in tune. He wrote new songs about Teddy, pieces he played on the beach and in after hour bars. His lyrics provided a civics lesson, addressed the collapse of our economic landscape, Teddy's looting of our domestic markets, factories and farms peddled to foreign investors, unemployment and double digit inflation leaving basic staples unaffordable, the middle class pushed toward poverty and the poor over the edge. Young aspirants sought Emilo's counsel. He taught them the art of making explosives from fertilizer, gunpowder out of potassium nitrate, charcoal and sulfur, and dynamite from ammonium nitrate and nitro-cellulose. When the sky above the capital exploded now in high streaks of orange and grey, Emilo and his friends played Bruce Cockburn's 'If I Had A Rocket Launcher' in chords of G.

"Wake up!" he went to the window and shouted loudly at his neighbors. "Deaf, dumb and blind."

"I'm sure they're sleeping."

"Right. Head in the sand. Tail between their legs. Bend over, here comes Teddy! Hell," he raised the bottle. "All tucked away. Bad dreams, I hope they have. Deaf, dumb and blind," he repeated. "Someone needs to wake them. All these nervous rabbits." He leaned outside the window and yelled, "Do you hear?" then waited to see if any lights came on. When nothing happened, he pulled himself back in and clicked his tongue.

I pointed toward the chair, told him to sit. "You're drunk."

"I am for sure," he blew into the top of the bottle until the neck whistled. "And tomorrow when I'm sober, what else will have changed?"

We both looked out the window then. Everything was pitch black beyond the light inside the apartment. I rubbed my head, felt the stubble coming in, thought of what Gandhi said about revolution, the rules for noncooperation and civil disobedience and how "Brute force will avail against brute force only when it is proved that darkness can dispel darkness." I started talking about the Velvet Revolution of Czechoslovakia, Poland's Solidarity Movement, the teachings of Nelson Mandela, America's Thoreau and Dr. Martin Luther King, but Emilo stopped me.

"Babble, babble, babble. The only way to deal with a mad dog is to give him a smack of the stick," he extended his arm, turned his free thumb and forefinger into a gun. "You want to get rid of a snake in the grass," he cocked his hand and pretended to shoot, then raised the bottle in his other hand and began singing the second verse of 'Junta Heartache.'

I went and took the anisette from him, put it on the table by his chair and motioned to his bedroom. "You need to call it a night. There's nothing more to do. I have to get home and sleep. I've work in the morning."

"Do you now?" Emilo went and sat in his chair, picked up his guitar. He was right, of course, my business was in no better shape than his shop, Teddy having undercut my margin of profit by forming his own agency, run as a State owned protection racket, demanding payments to bond against harm. Bameritans who did not pay wound up collecting on the policies I held for them. "It's all too ironic," Emilo strummed high C.

I said nothing, squeezed his shoulder and went downstairs. As I headed through the shop I heard him playing Dylan. "All the tired horses in the sun/How am I supposed to get any ridin' done?" Outside three urchins were poking through the trash, two boys and a girl, each thin-limbed and long-haired. They glanced up as I approached, hesitated for only a second then ran between the buildings and disappeared. Ten minutes later I turned onto my street, eager for sleep. Katima would be there, I knew, waiting for me at home, a recent arrangement, a reality that made me quicken my stride. I didn't want to think of anything more and purposely avoided picturing Emilo in his apartment after I left, convinced all would be better tomorrow.

There is a clipping on my tower which describes political prisoners in Uganda, Liberia and Iran using black and white strings to stitch their faces in protest of their circumstance. Emilo has read the article, has seen the photograph, has stood with me in front of my tower and said "Can you imagine that shit?"

Tomorrow I will learn how Emilo went back to the window and called again to his neighbors "Deaf, dumb and blind." I will picture him moving to his bedroom, fishing through his dresser drawers until he finds the small sewing kit with needle and thread. In the bathroom next, he'll run the needle under hot water, dry the end with three quick shakes and feed the thread into the hole. The first push passes upward through the underbelly of his bottom lip, breaking the skin and coming out the other side. He'll pull the thread around, in and out and back down, his mouth closed with four crude stitches. Additional threads will be used to close each ear, Emilo's eyelids pierced and sewn to the puffy brown flesh beneath. Deaf, dumb and blind, he wants them to see. In the dark, he'll turn and follow the walls with his hands, make his way down the stairs to the stoop outside where he'll sit and wait for people to find him.

CHAPTER 2

Milton Jabber kneels and works his hands between the toes of the dead boy. His fingers are strong from years of experience. He grips and bends the boy's feet, rolls and washes the arch and heel, removes the dirt and flakes of skin. The floor is a cool grey slab made slippery by the wash water. A small pool fills the center of the room, three feet deep and bordered by white slate. Wooden buckets, plastic sheets, soaps and bowls and bags of cotton are spread nearby.

Yesterday soldiers raided Abel Morkin's farm, accused him of giving milk and meat to NBDF rebels gathering again in the hills, and beat him to death with the butts of their rifles. Abel's family brought the boy's remains to the body washer that morning, a fragment of bone having passed through the red muscled center of Abel's heart, his flesh marked by black welts, gashes and clots of dried blood. Milton finishes with the feet and moves up the legs. He works in silence, dips a brown bucket back into the pool of water, sprinkles camphor inside, uses a round sponge to swab Abel's right arm.

A pumice stone scrapes away scales and scabs before powdered soap is applied. The narrow gutter surrounding the room flows with bloody water. Two windows, each round and no larger than a porthole, sit high up the far wall. The sunlight through the windows reflects off the pool. The cleansing takes three hours. Milton's meticulous and inspects his work several times. When he's finished, he uses a clean sheet and wraps Abel gently before signalling the family to come and take the boy away. Another body is already waiting, with a third to arrive at 4 o'clock. Milton rinses his hands in a separate sink, then goes next door, sits in the kitchen and eats the chicken salad his wife's made for him.

Kart Jabber arrives and joins his father at the table, watches the older man eat. "Busy day."

Milton nods in the direction of his work area.

"Teddy will make you a rich man yet."

"The General and others," he eyes his son. Last night, a few hours after the demolition of Emilo's shop, a pipe bomb exploded at Delistone's Bistro. The restaurant was crowded with soldiers, the bomb thrown through the front window. Luci Ferre had just finished singing a line from an American pop classic, "Don't it always seem to go, that you don't know what you got till it's gone," when flashes of orange appeared in the sky. Milton says nothing for several seconds, then asks. Kart leans back in his chair. His father shakes his head, pushes his lunch away, wipes his mouth with a hand that smells perpetually of camphor and harsh soap. He tries to counsel his son about restraint, refers to the consequence of impulse and the aftermath he's paid to wash clean.

"Who's seen more?" he starts to say, but a knock keeps him from continuing. Five people are waiting on the stoop out front, three of them in costume. American style zoot suits from the 1920's, one green and two yellow jackets with matching pants, pin-striped, dangling pocket chains, broad painted ties and Stetson Temple fur felt fedoras. The men introduce themselves as relatives of a boy killed last night in the blast, and ask of the body washer, "We would like you to prepare him."

"Of course," Milton has the dead boy brought next door. Kart waits only until the men go and remove the boy's body from the back of a blue station wagon before turning to his father. "What are you doing?"

"They've come to me."

"So? He's a soldier."

"The boy is dead."

"As he should be."

"That's enough," Milton leaves his son and begins walking to his work area. The other men carry the body next door. Kart stares at the bare feet of the dead boy sticking from the black plastic tarp, the irony a burlesque. He rubs his face, his own hands with a strong scent, not of camphor but sulphur. He remembers a night earlier that month when he and Kara and Angeline snuck in and waded through the cool shallow waters of his father's pool. Naked and softly splashing, their play seemed no more profane than the waters being used to cleanse dead soldiers.

Kart goes around back to where his mother's working in the garden. Mariene Jabber is a round woman with dark hair and large tea cup eyes. She's wearing her assigned costume as an American flapper in short skirt, turned-down hose and powdered knees. "Kart," she smiles and drives her hoe into the earth, churning the soil as he comes to kiss her cheek. "I know," she tells him, and he thinks for a moment she means about the Bistro, but she complains instead about her outfit, how she's scheduled to be on Burine Avenue in twenty minutes. She says to him then with a mix of both embarrassment and aggravation, "Isn't it though, by this point now, all so ridiculous?"

———

Teddy sits on the side of a large Louis XVI ottoman, the cushions flat beneath him, stuffed with the down of ducklings imported from Argentina. He leans back, raises his right leg, says "Come here girl and help me with my boots."

She is twenty, wearing a Little Bo Peep outfit, minus the leg muffs, the hemline cut just above her calf, the colors white and blue. Teddy runs a hand up under the girl's dress as she turns and bends over him. The camera mounted high in the corner is already recording as Teddy flips the hem, finds the warm seam between Bo Peep's cheeks, massages the fold and squeezes her rump. He slaps her bottom as she frees his foot. "Hooray for Hollywood," he whoops. "Let's see if you pass the audition."

In bare feet Teddy stands just over five feet seven inches, the lifts he wears in the heels of his boots adding four inches, altering his stride to something resembling a stumble. During his six years on TV, Teddy starred in Bamerita's top rated television show, 'General Admission,' a half hour comedy parodying the private and workday life of General Cornelius Hedgwaller following the War of the Winds. Dismissed from the army, Cornelius wound up taking a job as a maitre d' at the Steerway To Heaven Steakhouse. Teddy's natural capacity for farce and his ability to convey Cornelius' struggles adjusting to a newly liberated Bamerita gave 'General Admission' its appeal, was always good for a laugh.

At the height of his popularity Teddy left TV and took his act to the stage, where he presented a stand-up routine as the General. The audiences roared as Teddy in costume delivered jokes about the good old days when the military ruled and people had a healthy respect for authority. He praised the benefits of totalitarianism and the luxury of going to bed at night knowing everyone was well watched over. Members of the GRA - the Greater Republic Alliance - invited Teddy to join their group, offered specific ideas to improve his act. Speechwriters and image consultants were hired. Teddy began playing the largest venues in Bamerita, his shows recorded, quoted in the papers and broadcast on TV. At the time of the coup, Teddy's act had evolved to a point where few people thought of him anymore as the man from 'General Admission,' but saw him solely as Bamerita's newest ruler and face of the GRA.

For dinner that night Teddy wore his brown Prussian boondockers, the boots climbing his shin, causing his pants to billow below the knee. Joining him were the American Consul Eric Dukette, Chief Inspector Franco Warez, Father Amiel Piote, and Everett Doyle from the Ministry of Internal Planning. Teddy greeted his guests with a high salute, the medals pinned to the front of his faux General's uniform jangling as he marched. Two soldiers dressed in dark suits and white gloves served Cornish hens, boiled potatoes and German ale. Father Piote licked his lips and offered a blessing for the poor.

"A toast," Teddy raised his glass. "To Leo Covings," he told the others his news, how after much negotiation the American director had agreed to come to Bamerita. Hearty congratulations were extended. "Obviously Covings appreciates your talent, General."

"If not for your gift," Father Piote peeled the skin from his hen.

Teddy disputed none of this, pressed his knife against the bone of his bird and said to the Chief Inspector, "Let's keep an eye on things, shall we? We don't want any foolishness while our guest is here."

"No foolishness," Chief Inspector Warez promised.

"All this nonsense lately."

"They're making much of nothing."

"Good Baby is good business."

"Caveat emptor."

"If it will help them feel better," Teddy said, "we'll have someone arrested. One of the factory managers should do." He lifted a wing from the bird torn apart. The dining room table was plaited in a braided cane, the entire villa modeled after a chateau built in the Bavarian hills with pine panelling and a light jade color scheme, the halls filled with cactus plants in majolica pots. Everett Doyle wore a seal skin jacket, suggested "For safe measure more guards should be assigned to the daily shoots while Covings is here."

"A good idea. We don't want anything unseemly caught on film."

"No."

"Of course not."

"We wouldn't want to give the wrong impression."

"Film provides more than impression," Teddy corrected. "It creates reality."

"Which is exactly what we're doing."

"What we're doing, yes."

"Only a government that is truly progressive would even consider what we've done," Teddy sopped up the grease on his plate with a piece of bread. "Why is it so hard for them to understand?"

"Putting each Bameritan on film shows how broad-minded we are."

"How liberal."

"Ha! Yes. Everyone has their chance to be a star."

"Why do they fight it so?"

"Change is most vigorously resisted among the less enlightened," the good Father touched the cross on his papal chain.

"What do these people know?" Everett Doyle sliced his potato. "They've no idea how hard it is to run a government. They read of democracy in comic books and think everything is milk and honey."

"Your American founders understood, didn't they, Eric?" Teddy addressed the American Consul. "The framers of your constitution knew pure democracy was an unnatural form of government, that people benefited most when lead by the few." He leaned into the table then and recited from memory, "I believe further that a democratic Government is likely to be administered for a course of years, and can only end in Despotism when the people shall become so corrupted as to need despotic Government, being incapable of any other." Pleased with himself, he asked the American Consul, "Do you know who wrote that?" and answered before anyone else could. "None other than your Benjamin Franklin, that's who!"

Eric Dukette waited a moment, wondering if he should correct Teddy on the meaning of the Franklin quote, and deciding not to, he glanced around the table before replying, "It's good to see your sense of governing is so deeply rooted in American history, General."

"Deeply, yes," Teddy back in his room, repeats for the girl. "Smile for the camera," he turns her around, has her dance up on her toes, her dress lifted above her hips, waved left and right. Teddy sings, "She heaved a sigh and wiped her eye." Without his boots the cuffs of his pants droop several inches around his ankles. He bends his knees, slides forward. Bo Peep is in front of him and the camera's rolling. He removes his undershorts and puts his hands on the girl's head, touches her firmly. "With the throne," he says "comes the scepter," and offering his royal truncheon groans, "God bless America, but don't I know? That's a girl. That's it. That's all there is. Governing is no more than this. It's simply a matter of taking what I give you."

CHAPTER 3

I first met Katima after hurting my leg in a fall. This was last winter. Before then, between losing Tamina and now, my relationships with women were limited, in large part, to casual dinners and the occasional act of physical cooperation between ladies Emilo sent my way. I didn't subscribe to the Brahmacharya's idea of celibacy as a means of enhancing spiritual enlightenment, but kept to myself as a matter of course. My abstinence was practiced aggressively and with periods of absolute commitment that had nothing to do with Gandhi and everything to do with the world as I found her and being still in love with Tee.

I lived with my children, and then alone, and walking home one night had absentmindedly stumbled over the curb. Following a period of resting my knee, Dr. Bernarr recommended I swim at the University's pool. Because of my injury and lack of stamina, I could manage little more than splashing and slapping at the water. I stopped after a few laps, breathing hard and holding onto the side as Katima came over and knelt on the deck.

"What are you doing?" she wanted to know if the problem with my leg was trauma or a more permanent condition. "You move like a boat with one oar."

I told her about my fall and she instructed me to quit doing laps. "You're not ready," she explained the key to recovery was isolating my injury and working the muscles. "With laps, you have your arms and one good leg to compensate." She had me raise my legs behind me and float to the surface, my hands still holding onto the side of the pool. "Kick," she said. I did as told, felt immediately the extra exertion. "Do six sets of thirty seconds each. Rest fifteen second in between. Count them off like this," she showed me how to breath.

Ten minutes later I got out of the water, my legs spent and not completely stable beneath me. Katima was off in the far end of the pool, overseeing the exercise of four other people, as I shuffled along the deck toward the locker room. I showered and went home. The next afternoon I returned to the pool where I found Katima swimming laps alone. As I began my kicking exercise, she swam to where I was and asked, "How's the knee?"

"Good. Better, thank you."

Beads of water ran down her cheeks into the dimples at the corners of her mouth. I let go of the side, allowed my feet to settle on the shallow bottom as she climbed out of the water and removed her silver swim cap. Her brown hair fell just over her ears. She shook her cap, dangled her toes from the edge, said "I thought that might be you," as

37

we introduced ourselves. I asked clumsily if we had met before and she, in turn, teased me with, "Don't you remember?"

"I'm sorry."

"Don't be," she laughed. "We haven't. But people know who you are."

She stepped back, glanced at the camera which was anchored above the exit sign on the north end of the pool. Cameras not involved in the day's scheduled shoot ran randomly, making it impossible to tell whether or not we were being recorded. "André Mafante and Katima Hynne at the pool, take one," she smiled and made as if opening and closing one of those clapboards directors used when filming. "Would you like to say a few words to Teddy?"

"You shouldn't taunt him," I warned as she pointed again at the camera. "It isn't worth the trouble."

"A few words," she ignored me, and pretending to hold a microphone, said "This is your chance to go on record."

"But I am on record."

"Right," she nodded and put her left heel in a small puddle. "Then I'll go first. Ask me anything."

"For the record?"

"Sure."

"How is it you know so much about treating my leg?"

"It's what I do," she splashed at me with the side of her foot. "Physical therapy. I used to work at the hospital before Teddy threw me out. It seems our government doesn't value therapy and refuses to employ nursemaids to bend knees and rub bellies," she quoted the language one such actuary from the Ministry of Health used in his report. "Now I see patients privately and Teddy taxes what I earn at 60%." She shook her head at the absurdity, joked about 'General Admission,' and how, "At least when Teddy was on TV we could change the channel."

"There was that," I shifted my sore leg underwater. Katima remained above me. I could see her green eyes reflecting the pale blue of the water. She reached down and stirred the waters with two fingers, said "My turn."

"Alright."

"About your tower," she asked me then, "Is it true?" and wanted to know about Tamina.

I sank beneath the surface until just my head was exposed, and placing my hands once more on the side, raised my legs, stretched my body until I was floating. "I should finish my exercises," I put my face in the water, just deep enough so that my breathing became a struggle. I stayed this way, kicking and holding on, until Katima left the pool.

Outside, after my shower, I walked home slowly on my sore leg. Katima caught up with me as I came across Deveh Street, halfway between my house and the University. She was riding a red bike, her gym bag clipped to a rack over her rear tire, and slowing down to pace herself beside me, said "I didn't mean to be insensitive. I tend to blurt things out." She apologized again for her reference to Tee. "I'm sorry if I put my foot in it. What I meant to say is that I think your tower's fantastic. We should all build monuments."

Dressed in a blue t-shirt and beige shorts, her hair still wet and combed straight, she straddled the sides of her bike, started talking briefly then about my work at Bameritan Samaritan, only to stop suddenly and confide her own story. "I was thirteen during the War of the Winds. My father was a farmer, a supporter of Kenefie. At night sometimes NBDF rebels came from the hills and asked for food which we gave them. One morning, we found a wounded soldier in our garden. My father carried him into the house, cleaned and stitched the hole in his side. The man had a high fever and slept for several days.

"When the rebels came again, my father refused to let them take the soldier away. There was an argument and one of the men went to the bed and grabbed the soldier by his arm, reopening his wound. My father stopped him, covered the soldier's side with his fingers, shouted at the others to remember what we were fighting for. Eventually they backed away, agreed to interrogate the soldier at our house, and convinced he was of no use to them, left after an hour with six sacks of our food.

"The War ended and the NBDF offered amnesty. My father drove the soldier to the hospital." Katima squeezed the handlebars on her bike. "A week later three policemen showed up at our farm and charged my father with aiding the enemy. The complaint was eventually dropped, but neighbors and merchants would no longer deal with us. My father said nothing in his defense. Our farm failed and he found a job as an apprentice cobbler under a false name. That winter he worked in a basement cutting old leather treated in formaldehyde. A lung infection spread to his heart and killed him the following spring. My mother had family in Veritone and we went to live with my uncle. When I enrolled at the University four years later, I learned half my tuition was paid for by a one-time soldier working then in Gabaroon. 'To cover what was covered,' the note he wrote said."

Katima moved the front tire of her bike back and forth. "We all have stories, don't we, André?"

It was true, I knew, and this I told her. "About Tamina," I began, but she stopped me by putting the wheel of her bike against my right leg, and changing the subject, asked "Do you ride?"

"What? No."

"Not ever?"

"I haven't in years."

"But you can?" she patted the seat, reached for my briefcase. "It's better than walking for your leg."

"I don't think," I stepped away, only Katima insisted, "It will all come back to you. It's like riding a bike," she laughed and leaned the handlebars into my hip. I objected twice more, was outargued each time, and finally gave in. My balance was a wobble, leaving me to pedal cautiously while Katima trotted alongside. "You're doing great," she cheered, watching as I maneuvered up the hill and down again into my drive. I set the bike by my front porch and walked to the curb where I waited for Katima who was just then coming over the hill. "You see? I told you," she handed me back my briefcase. "Piece of cake. How's the leg?"

"It feels good."

"You should ride more often," she encouraged me, smiled as I told her about the old brown three-speed of Ali's still out back. The top of my tower rose above the rooftops. I thought of inviting Katima for a drink, in appreciation for treating my leg, but felt uneasy and said instead, "Yes, well, I should get inside. I have some work. There are things I need to do."

Katima pretended not to hear, and looking up at my tower, asked "Do you mind?" She followed the path around my side lawn into the backyard where I watched her disappear for a moment behind the tower. The shadows in the yard passed over my house and through the kitchen window as Katima came back around and stood in front of me. I lowered my eyes, said "Yes, well, goodnight," and took two steps toward my house only to have my bad leg buckle.

As I stumbled, Katima caught my hand. "It's alright, André," she squeezed my fingers. "Really." She pointed up toward the top of my tower and the scaffolding secured by rods and hooks. "Look at that. The whole thing is nothing but a dangle. All of it, and yet every time you climb, you somehow make it back down." She did not release my hand, reminded me then of yesterday at the pool, how she explained the necessity for isolating my injury, the importance of learning to relax, float and kick, the exertion difficult yet healing. "You hold on, and then you let go, and before you know it you're like a fish swimming in water again."

—

I did not get home from Emilo's until 1:00 a.m., and dog tired, slipped into bed. Katima slept with her arms spread half on my side of the sheet. I called her twice that evening to let her know what was happening, and glad to be home, I stroked her hair. She stirred and reached, and still asleep, embraced me.

When the alarm went off, I moved stiffly, hung over and sore from all the lifting done at Emilo's last night. Katima fixed tea and toast while I

STEVEN GILLIS

showered under cold water which did little more than chill my aching head. We parted with plans to meet for a late lunch, and exhausted still, I debated taking my car or riding my bike to work. I usually followed Roland Avenue through the Plaza to my office, stopping to knock on Emilo's door, but this morning I assumed he'd be dozing off the effects of the anisette, and stayed on the numbered boulevards before arriving at my building just south of the University.

The roads in the capital were rutted and rattled the wheels of my bike. During Dupala's first term in office, the streets were sealed with an oil based tar manufactured in Bamerita. Two years ago, under Teddy, an American company was contracted to add an additional layer of gilsonite. Special international loans were provided to cover the cost, money Teddy appropriated and deposited in private accounts. The gilsonite acquired was low grade, the roads now grooved and split through much of the capital and beyond. I spent the morning handling claims, reviewing my financial figures, trying to determine how close my business was to going under. People came early, family members of the dead or injured, beneficiaries in need of their checks. I phoned Emilo around noon but got no answer. A few minutes later, Davi Suntu poked his head inside my office and said, "We need to talk."

I'd known Davi since our student days, was there as he planned and subsequently founded Suntu Husbandry and Farming Group. The Group leased wasteland for the raising of chickens and pigs, expanded in time into food processing, corn and vineyards. When Teddy overthrew Dupala, Davi's taxes were tripled, tariffs attached to the Group's contracts, bribes and kickbacks imposed as the cost

43

of doing business. Rather than be bullied out of the market, Davi created Suntu Savings and Loan which secured private capital to keep the Group solvent. Unamused, Teddy had the Ministry of Treasure file false charges against Davi, Suntu S&L and the Group. A series of hearings followed. Our friend Josh Durret provided legal counsel, guided Davi through the catalog of corruption in Teddy's courts.

Three minutes after Davi arrived we were driving south toward the Plaza, the ruts in the road bouncing us hard on the seats. Along the way I struggled with what Davi told me, touched my mouth, ears and eyes, angry with myself for having left Emilo alone last night. "I should have stayed with him."

Davi's large brown buddha face was wet with sweat as he tried to comfort me. "You couldn't have known."

"But that's just it." Word of Emilo's protest had already reached Teddy who ordered his soldiers to remove him from the street. Rather than toss him in jail and be done however, a different strategy was imposed, a plan to make a mockery of his effort. As we entered the Plaza, I could see Emilo up on the makeshift platform the soldiers had constructed that morning. The wooden stage was set on the north side, Emilo there in a metal chair, his t-shirt and jeans removed, replaced with a green zoot suit and black fedora. His image was projected onto the movie screen, the white threads running through his lips, his eyelids and ears clearly visible. Dancing girls in flapper skirts and sheer white hose kicked in a row behind the chair and across the stage.

44

Davi parked his car close to the platform, near to where Mical Delmont, Ryle Naceme, Josh Durret and Don Pendar were already standing. The Plaza was an open space, shadeless with shops at the perimeter and Teddy's enormous screen on the far east side. People passing through the Plaza stared at Emilo and hurried off. The dancing girls skipped to the music crackling from an overhead speaker, an old recording of 'Thoroughly Modern Millie' playing loudly. A man in a truck worked the remote controlled cameras mounted overhead. I ran from the car and climbed up on the stage, called to Emilo, "It's me. Can you hear? Emilo, man," I felt in my pockets for something to cut the strings.

"We tried," Josh called from below. "He won't let us."

"Come on, Emilo," I squeezed his arms, did my best to get him to his feet. "It's ok. Davi's brought his car. There's no soldiers. We can leave any time."

Instead of standing, Emilo pulled away, shifted his weight and locked his hands beneath the chair.

"What are you doing?"

He tightened his hold. I leaned closer. "Listen to me. This won't work, this thing you've done. Deaf, dumb and blind, I understand, but don't you get it? Teddy wants people to think he did this to you. He brought you here to confuse everyone, to have them believe stitching your face was his idea. The point you want to make, Teddy won't let you. It's over. Come on."

Emilo shook his head, his features altered to a rag doll state. I stood over him and repeated, "What good does it do for you to stay when no one knows what really happened?"

He reached for me then and touched my hip.
"Sure. Me, yes. But I can't very well explain
to everyone."
Emilo again, made as if he was typing.
"It won't work. Emilo, listen to me."
Don Pendar approached the stage from street
level. In khaki shorts, his long legs thick like
walking sticks, his features abrupt and angular,
cut across the bone. A disciple of Emilo's, such
extremes as this were a sweet crystal rush for him.
He waved his hands and said, "It has to work."
I knew better than to reply, bent down to
Emilo and said, "Listen to me."
"He knows," Don Pendar again, tapping the
stage. "We should all stitch our faces and sit
beside him."
"And after that?" I couldn't resist, turned
and stared toward the front of the platform. If he
was the enemy I might have known what to do, but
Don Pendar was a friend, his youth and innocence
a bad combination, like pouring nitroglycerin on
a bowl of shredded wheat. A professor at the University, hired just before the coup, he was working
on a series of articles covering Bameritan culture
and the history of revolution which he planned to
turn into a book. For some time now he came to
speak with me, intrigued by my passivity, the role
I played in founding the NBDF, in the War of the
Winds and Bameritan Samaritan, about Gandhi and
my tower, and how was it I actually believed
anything could be achieved without rebellion.
"Crazy," he said when I tried to explain.
We sat at night over drinks and debated the many
ways to sustain a free and democratic Bamerita.
Well read, he offered endless quotes from William
Mackenzie, Sun Tzu, Minni Arcua Minnawi and

46

Subcommander Marcos. "If we let him stay," he argued again. "If we stay with him."
"Then what?"
"Then?" he seemed genuinely perplexed by my question. "Then Teddy won't win."
His reply made no sense. "What does that mean? Won't win what? How does Emilo staying in the Plaza accomplish anything?"
"André's right," Davi sat on the hood of his car, his plump legs folded beneath him, his round belly pressing against his white Beecher Island short sleeve shirt. "Now is not the time for puffing out our chests."
"We're his friends," I pointed back at Emilo. "We can't just leave him here and wait for something else to happen." The moment I said this a jeep sped into the Plaza and three soldiers jumped out.
Dressed the same as Emilo in zoot suits, black shirts and white ties, their rifles now Tommy guns, their boots were covered by yellow spats. I was knocked from the platform to the street. The music changed to ragtime, the dancing girls kicked up their legs while the soldiers grabbed Emilo on either side, his wrists and ankles tied to the chair, his boots and socks pulled off. A long brown feather was removed from inside the shirt of the largest soldier who came around in front of Emilo, turned his head and spoke directly to the camera. "So you thought you'd get away with it, did ya?" He delivered his line as if already in the middle of a scene, and bending over began tickling Emilo's feet.
I saw Emilo clench his jaw, straining not to laugh. Tears slipped through the stitching of his eyes, his body shaking and bobbing up and down

as he drew his lips in hard against the threads. The second soldier stood behind the chair, wiggling his fingers beneath Emilo's arms. I shouted along with the others while the third soldier raised his gun and drove us back. "Buddy, Buddy," the first soldier shook his head, tossed away the feather and replaced it with a silver hammer. "Did you really think?"

I cried out, unable to do more, watching as the soldier took aim at Emilo's right foot and brought the hammer down.

———

My father's house is a half mile from the Plaza, just east of the University, a mile south of where I live. Don Pendar hurried with me across Havarine Avenue, asked several times if I'd seen enough. "Now, André? Now?" He danced out in front of me, the question predictable. "Your best friend."

"My best friend would want me to keep my head."

"Use your head is more like it. If you understood history."

"I do understand," I found myself arguing more than I wanted. "Our response to Teddy can't be rash." I listed then the recent demonstrations in Bolivia, Nigeria and Venezuela, Tbilisi, Georgia, Argentina and Nepal, where nonviolent populist movements brought about social and political change.

"If those are your examples," Don Pendar interrupted. "In the countries you name the crisis is ongoing."

"That's not true," I grew more adamant. "There's a dialogue between the governments and the people. Open democratic elections are in the works."

"Assuming that's the case," again Don Pendar waved me off, "there's still no dialogue in Bamerita. And no democracy."

"None of which gives us license to commit violence." I tried a different tact, threw out the names of the Lord's Resistance Army in Uganda, the Maoist guerrillas in New Delhi and the NLD in Myanmar, warned Don Pendar against treating anarchy as a panacea, a comment he was also quick to reject.

"We're not anarchists. It's not anarchy when the government is illegitimate. Are you forgetting already?" and here he pulled from my own pocket the bloody cloth I used after the hammer crashed through Emilo's foot.

The first blow had shattered bone, Emilo's toes, medial and lateral cuneiform all splintered and driven into the wood. The second blow flattened his left foot, brought pieces of pale white cartilage poking through the skin, pulverized like brittle sticks in a fleshy sock. Twice more the hammer fell. The dancing girls abandoned their kicks, covered their eyes and mouths in actual horror while the two remaining soldiers turned their heads. On the screen Emilo was shown locking his jaw, struggled against the ropes, his head snapping back until his shoulders arched and pitched, and unable to hold out any longer he wailed. The threads in his mouth split his lips into four meaty sections, the pink flaps ripped and dangling, his eyelids torn and bloodied as we looked on.

The man inside the truck called, "Cut! That's a wrap! Perfect! Perfect!" The soldiers left the stage while the rest of us ran to undo Emilo's arms and legs and carried him to Davi's car. Don Pendar reached for my elbow as I wiped Emilo's face with

my handkerchief. "Let them go, André," he pulled
me out as Mical and Josh jumped into the car and
Davi prepared to drive to the hospital. "They have
him now. It's alright. We need to talk."

A quarter mile from my father's house, we
approached St. Murced Cathedral where a wedding
had just taken place. The bride and groom were
out front, cheered by their guests, everyone singing
and laughing, giddy in their celebration. At first
no one noticed the soldiers coming from behind
the church and entering the crowd. Don Pendar
and I stopped and watched from the opposite side
of the street as the soldiers spoke with the guests
and made them hand over envelopes with cash
intended for the new couple. Wrapped gifts were
carried from inside the church and loaded into a
jeep. A dozen street urchins stood off behind a
cannonball tree, eager to beg for coins, but seeing
the soldiers they stayed away.

Don Pendar was already three strides into
the street before I could run and grab his arm.
"Wait, wait," I redoubled my grip, dug my heels
into the pavement, said "Let me," followed by,
"See here. This is a church," and pointing up at
the Cathedral, did my best to draw the soldiers'
attention.

I spoke with false authority, said "There's a
wedding taking place. You can't steal these gifts." As
I did this, Don Pendar broke from my hold and lunged
toward the watch one of the soldiers had snatched
from a member of the wedding party. For his effort
he received a blow to the head. A cut opened above
his eye. I jumped in between, just as the soldier prepared to hit him again, and identifying myself, hoped
my name might mean something, only the soldier was
young and unsure. "Mafante? Mafante?"

"That's right." I repeated, "You can't," but my appeal produced a hard shove and an order to, "Move off!"

Don Pendar made as if he was about to start up again. I caught his sleeve and tugged him back across the street. "What were you thinking?"

"You shouldn't have stopped me," he gave this as his answer.

"No? And if I didn't? What did you expect would happen?"

"More than this," he wiped at his cut with the back of his hand. I dismissed his bravado, told him, "You've been watching too many old movies. You're not thinking clearly. Did it ever occur to you the soldiers might not appreciate your interfering? What if they shot the bride and groom in retaliation for your meddling? You do realize there are others around. You can't give into the first foolish impulse that comes to mind. There are things to consider beyond your adrenaline. You're being irresponsible. The consequence of your actions can't be reversed."

Don Pendar waited until I finished, and taking the already bloody handkerchief I handed him, dabbed at his cheek, turned and walked backwards in order to face me, lowered the cloth and used his index finger to trace the welt he received when struck. "You're right, André," he said. "There are always consequences, for whatever we do or don't do each time."

———

My father is a large man, built along the lines of a heavyweight wrestler, stout through the chest and belly, with thick calves and massive thighs.

He remains our patriarchal presence, his mind as keen as ever, the articles he writes and advice he gives those who come and seek his counsel top drawer. Age has nonetheless diminished much of his strength, his health at seventy-four is suspect. After my mother died, my father's diet gave way to meals of sweet yams, Ho-Ho's and canned sardines in a mustard sauce. "At my age," he said, "it's important to find a certain comfort in all forms of sustenance."

He called Don Pendar over as we came into the den, asked "What happened to your face?" The welt on Don Pendar's cheek had started to color, the blood clotting around the gash. I explained about the soldiers at the church and my father sighed, "For once it's good you have a hard head."

The den in my father's house is lined with books, the shelves stacked to the ceiling, a wheeled ladder he can no longer use pushed to the left. Texts out of reach are retrieved with a long wooden pole, the books tumbling down and remaining in piles after they're read. My father sat in his leather chair, the sides of him spread out like a magnificent old walrus. Word of what happened to Emilo made its way quickly through the capital, bringing more men to fill my father's house. Such meetings were common now, the frustration and anticipation of dealing with Teddy palpable, a matter I feared of no longer when but how.

My father folded his hands across his middle. Ali arrived as I was in the kitchen getting ice to put on Don Pendar's cheek. (Anita, my daughter, was in America this past year, completing her graduate studies.) My son has sandy hair, curled and brushed back from his eyes. His frame is thin. A teacher along with his girlfriend, Feona Dumarre, at All Kings Middle School, Ali wore jeans and sandals and a t-shirt with a quote from Lincoln: "Whatever you are, be a good one."

Recently, as fallout from Teddy's failed economic policies continued to gnaw away at our collective center, children half-starved and far from home, orphans and runaways, flocked to the capital, seeking food and shelter. Teddy called the children road rats, quoted the writings of Jefferson: "It's not the duty of government to extend charity." Soldiers were ordered to chase the children from our streets, the Plaza and parks and alleys between our shops. Last month Ali and Feona began sneaking children into All Kings at night. Food was gathered in a daily scramble, the gymnasium used for sleeping until the day students arrived. "You have your mother's way of doing things," I told my son. "You have her sensibilities and stubbornness. You and your sister." Those who knew Tamina told Ali the same. "You have your mother's eyes. Her laugh. You have her look within you."

Ali joined me in the kitchen, asked about Emilo, wanted to know details. I set the tray of ice down, filled a glass with water. My hands, I realized, were trembling. Ali took the tray and began dumping the ice into a plastic sandwich bag. "What now?" he asked.

"I'm not sure."

"You think?"

"Something, yes," I sipped my water, heard through the open kitchen door Gari Charuf, Zak Frazor, Jeri Fulan and Moriz Schwin joining the others. By the time Ali and I returned to the den, Don Pendar was in full riff, addressing the group. "What we need is to coordinate our attack with those already in the hills and work our offensive

53

from the inside out." Half the room bobbed their heads. I handed over the bag of ice, waited for everyone to settle down. "An attack is certainly one possibility," I began my scramble, was thinking of Emilo, and of Katima, of history repeating and what any sort of redundancy would mean for us now. "I agree the time has come," I gave them this, spoke as if there could be no doubt, then said, "But there are better ways to deal with Teddy than starting a war."

"Come on, André," Ryle Naceme cut me off. Zak Frazor whistled loud. Moriz Schwin groaned, while Don Pendar held the ice against his cheek and waved his free hand in a circle. "We've been all over this before."

In past meetings, it was true, for some time now. "So much the better," I glanced at my father for support. "We can get down to details then."

Gari Charuf, the ex-union official, insisted we not waste our time, though Edd Heff and Jeri Fulan, the chemist, said "Let's hear André out."

"It won't work," Moriz Schwin stared at Ali. I tapped the top of my father's desk gently until everyone looked back at me. "Not only will it work, it has worked, just recently in Venezuela and Nigeria, and earlier with Gandhi in South Africa and in Ahmedabad, and with Alina Pienkowska in Poland. If you understood history," I couldn't resist repeating the slight Don Pendar used earlier, and described in detail what Gandhi called 'hartals,' said "All things considered, a national strike is our most effective strategy."

"You can't be serious," Don Pendar set the bag of ice at his feet. "What good is a strike if Teddy still controls the army?"

"That's just it. That's the whole point," I

grew nervous but pressed on. "A strike makes the army irrelevant. If we stick together, there's nothing Teddy can do." I listed then our supporters, the workers at the factories and canneries, truck drivers and shoremen, shopowners and farmers all canvased in the weeks before and ready to strike. I mentioned again the expediency with which Gandhi organized his first hartals, how he, too, encouraged everyone to stick together and the success he had. "If we shut down the sale of raw materials and manufactured goods, the trade of fungible produce and exporting of our ore, bauxite and tin, we can neutralize Teddy's power and drive him out of office."

"So you say, but how do you suppose?" Zak Frazor indexed the flaws in my plan, all the risk for arrest and worse. A few drops of water escaped from the plastic bag on the floor. I went and put my hands behind my father's chair and replied in turn, "We know what will happen otherwise. Teddy's just waiting for us to gather our rifles and pitchforks and what sort of plan is that?"

"It's the only plan," Don Pendar placed his boot atop the bag of ice. Several men hooted and cawed while others encouraged me to go on. "What about the movie?" Jak Kleer wanted to know.

"The movie, most definitely," I told them. "We'll boycott that as well."

"I'm for it," Edd Huff in a sailor's suit said.

"A strike is our best option," I repeated.

"The best laid plans," Gari Charuf mocked.

Morus Hunds agreed with me. "Business is always the root." "Money is the core."

"If we cut Teddy off at the source."

"It's true."

"If we can."

"A strike then?" Ali called for a vote, while Don Pendar reminded everyone of Emilo, argued again in favor of a more aggressive attack. We debated this way for some time, until Jeri Fulan and Ryle Naceme turned and asked, "What do you think, Gabriel Mafante?"

My father rolled his head forward. No pacifist, I knew he wouldn't reject the idea of revolution simply because I asked. Still, he'd grown impatient waiting for those who supported an open rebellion to present a viable plan, and flicking his fingers across his belly said, "I think for now a strike works best." He raised his chin so that the folds in his neck parted, exposing the inner seam of fleshy creases. "We could, of course, schedule another meeting and discuss the matter further, evaluate again the pros and cons, examine both sides, make a list, take our time, conduct a study and put our findings through a committee. Or we can accept that a strike is a sufficient choice for now and focus on what needs to be done."

I remained beside my father's chair, relieved by his endorsement, however much it came with reservation. The others glanced among themselves, and deferring to my father, turned their attention back to me. "What now then?" they asked.

"What now?" I also wondered.

Don Pendar stood across the room, the bruise on his face a purplish-red. His anger clear, he came toward me, leaned in and whispered, "Congratulations. It's quite an achievement to mislead so many people this way. What do you expect to happen when we walk out of the factories, the docks and mines and water plant? The soldiers will enjoy themselves, won't they? A strike, André? Lambs to the slaughter. You think you're the only one with history? Jallianwalla Bagh, André. What makes you think you know best?"

I turned away, stopped listening and shifted my attention to the others and the work at hand. I spent the next half hour keeping myself busy with lists and assignments, answering questions and making calls, organizing what I could, who to contact and where to start, and when I did at last look up again Don Pendar was gone.

CHAPTER 4

Chief Inspector Warez's second wife, Casmola Gil Warez-Daumatero, wanted very much to be in Teddy's film. As an actress, she'd no appreciable training, her talents less artistic than corporeal, and still she had Warez ask Teddy to consider her for bigger parts. Twice now Teddy agreed to look her over. When Casmola heard about the American director, she insisted on meeting him. The Chief Inspector carried headshots and copies of Casmola's tapes in his car, promised to arrange an audition once Leo Covings reached the capital.

Tonight however, Warez was worn through and didn't want to talk of anything having to do with the American or Teddy's movie. A few short hours after the incident in the Plaza, a box marked 'Liquor' was carried into Mendola's Social Club and placed behind the bar. A girl named Tobbie HaHa was dancing for the soldiers to Chaka Kahn's, 'Tell Me Something Good,' when a blast blew chunks of her into the street. Warez spent much of his evening kicking through the rubble, the building in collapse, the light fixtures dangling from wires like the necks of dead swans.

Driving back through the Plaza, the Chief Inspector noticed the stage was gone, set ablaze and burned to the ground. Earlier, he had his men dismantle the stage but Teddy rescinded the order. "The platform's a great reminder. Let's leave her there." He instructed Warez to reassemble everything as it was before. In no time the stage was torched. Warez slowed his car, made sure the danger had passed and the fire wouldn't spread. He flicked his cigarette into the ash and went home.

Casmola was laying on the couch in the front room as he came in. A video of Bertolucci's 'The Dreamers,' which Warez bought his wife last week off a bootleg dealer was playing on the TV. "Which one was it?" she asked without moving her eyes from the screen.

"Mendola's."

"Harrhh. Why do they always hit the good ones?"

The Chief Inspector tossed his hat on the chair and removed his jacket. His clothes smelled of smoke. He slipped his holster from his shoulder, left it hanging on the knob of the door. The house was from his first marriage. His ex-wife, Valari Demil Warez-Blancar, was once a dancer, before the weight of middle age altered her figure and shifted her creative fires to a travelling seed broker from Vecine. Casmola was much younger, her career to date included two digital movies and a part in the serialized television drama, 'Tweener's Retreat.' (She appeared as Waitress #2.) A month after Valari left, Warez met Casmola at a Halloween ball where he came as Ivan the Conqueror and she a fille de joie. The Chief Inspector stood behind the couch, watched three actors - two boys and a girl in their early twenties - stare through a large black metal gate at a riot taking place in the street. 'The Dreamers' was set in France, 1968, during the second French Revolution. The reenactment was of the fighting between students, soldiers and police at Nanterre University, the Sorbone and the Boulevard St. Michel. So much violence upset the Chief Inspector. He pointed at the television and said of de Gaulle's closing Nanterre, "What did he expect?" After twenty-six years as a police officer, Warez was still amazed how ill-equipped most governments were at keeping the peace. Dictators always pulled the reins too tight until something snapped, while liberals misconstrued democracy for a license to relax civil law. Under both extremes order collapsed, further complicating Warez's ability to do his job.

"All things in moderation," he believed in asserting his authority with an even hand. That said, the function of the Chief Inspector was impossible to separate from Teddy Lamb. Warez tried absolving himself of accountability by insisting his violations were political and beyond the province of his office. The rationale failed. He knew of Good Baby before the truth got out, was in on plans to take care of Abel Morkin, Emilo Debar and others. The best he could do was tell himself things would be that much worse under a different Chief Inspector. It was at times sufficient comfort.

"This is what they make a movie about?" Warez shook his head, thought again of Mendola's, of Emilo and Abel and mentioned each to his wife. Casmola waved her hand and told her husband to, "Be quiet. I'm trying to listen."

The scene changed. Warez saw the three actors, naked then in their apartment, as removed from the fighting as Casmola on her couch. Tired, he rubbed at his face, considered a drink before bed. The light from the television caused half the room to glow. He ran a hand across the back of his neck, and looking at the litter of dishes and clothes, magazines and ashtrays overflowing, wondered if the chaos which had followed him home wasn't part of a pandemic. "About all this," he said to Casmola. "With how busy I am, and how little it seems you have to do, it would be nice to come in and find things a bit more tidy."

"It would be nice," Casmela held up her hand without turning her attention from the TV. The Chief Inspector stared at her fingers, wondered if she might listen better if he nibbled on them. "It's all filth," he said louder. "Do you think perhaps tomorrow?" He tried sounding less impatient and waited for his wife's response.

Casmela paused the video, annoyed at having her movie interrupted. "Tomorrow what, Frankie?"

"This mess."

"I know. It's too much, isn't it?" She sat up and tossed her head so that her hair dangled over the back of the couch. "I mean here you are, the Chief Inspector, and look how we live. Some days I get up and just want to scream. Who's to clean this mess now?" Warez gazed down at his wife, thought for a moment she must be joking. "Who you ask?" He moved away from the couch, stood for a second as the images on the TV came back to life, and turning, kicked off his boots and said to Casmola, "I'm going to bed. It's late and I've seen enough."

Our strike began three days after the meeting at my father's house. From the Port to the factories, to the markets and shops, people did not go into work. The mines were abandoned, the water plant closed, ships in the harbor without shoremen unable to dock. We quit our costumes, ran from the soldiers and refused to be filmed. Merchants and mechanics, waiters and store clerks, secretaries and laborers stayed home. To feed ourselves, we diverted our produce - grains and milk, eggs and meat and cheese - through an underground network of vendors. The government responded by raiding our farms, seizing our supplies and destroying our secret markets. Gas and utilities were rationed at triple the cost. (After one week the line to purchase government fuel and cooking oil exceeded two days wait.) Money lenders and sellers set up booths outside Teddy's banks, took advantage of our deflated currency by exchanging our assets for American dollars, marcs and euros and francs.

Despite the strain, our strike endured. Each night, at 8:00 p.m., we showed our solidarity by standing at the curbs and blowing whistles, clapping hands and beating loudly on metal pots. With my office closed, I spent my days riding about the capital on Ali's old brown bike, answering questions and offering support. A letter signed by my father, Davi Suntu, Paul Bernarr, Mical Delmont, Josh Durret and myself was sent to Teddy laying out our demands for ending the strike. Open elections and a permanent moratorium on filming headed the list. Instead of a reply, Teddy twice again raised the cost of electricity, water, oil and gas.

Each day soldiers on patrol made arrests. Shopkeepers, farmers and laborers were thrown into the back of jeeps and taken to Moulane Prison.

More men spoke of revolution then, quit the capital and joined the rebels in the hills. Emilo was released from the hospital with his feet inside thick plaster casts, his shattered bones held together by screws. His face re-stitched, gave him a permanently offended sort of scowl. I brought him food and drink in the morning and at night. As it hurt him still to move his lips, I was able to talk without interruption. "I think," I told him. "I believe," I said of the strike.

Even so, whenever I started in, my worry surfaced, the words catching clumsily in my throat. Emilo drank whiskey through a straw, listened to me stammer, pointed at my ears, my mouth and eyes and shook his head.

Katima and I sat in the kitchen late at night and compared notes about our day. Somehow the demands of our strike agreed with her. She slept little and ate less, yet appeared more fit than ever. Rising early, she rode about the capital on her own bike, worked with a group of women who coordinated the needs of families, making sure everyone had daily staples, medicines and clothes. I confided my concerns, counted on her to understand and rally my mood against my worst fears. When I said of our progress, "It feels as if we're beating at fires with straw brooms and sticks," she rubbed my cheek and answered, "Of course it does, André. What did you expect?"

Yesterday, Katima brought home four fresh oranges and cheese which she sliced and arranged on a plate. One by one we ate each piece. Afterward, we undressed upstairs and slipped into bed where I reached and touched her shoulder, the soft flesh near her breast. Her brown hair lay dark against the pillow. Making love, I didn't think of

Tamina the way I once did, first unavoidably and then more purposely until the need past, but held Katima while taking in the immediacy of the moment. I was still no less surprised that we had met at all that day at the pool, though things had settled in between us, the unexpectedness of my current happiness becoming less extreme, Katima's proximity now something I relied on.

Laying in the dark, I thought of a book I read recently, a history of the Solidarity Movement in Poland. Alina Pienkowska was a nurse at the Gdansk shipyard in 1980 who, along with Bogdan Borusewicz, Jacek Kuron and Lech Walesa, helped organize a protest after workers were fired unjustly from the yard. The remaining workers locked themselves behind the gates, refused to leave even as the government threatened to send soldiers in. Over the next few days dozens of other Polish factories went out on strike in support of Gdansk. Negotiations were contentious, but eventually the conflict between the shipyard and the government was resolved. As the workers celebrated and headed home, Alina turned to Walesa and shouted, "You betrayed them! Now the authorities will crush the others like bedbugs!" She accused the men of abandoning the factories still on strike. "Solidarity! Solidarity!" she shouted until all the workers returned to the yard.

The moon covered our bed through the window. I could see my tower in the glow across the way. On my dresser was a photograph of Tamina. I shifted closer to Katima, thought again of Alina, how despite the success of the Gdansk strike the communist government clung to power, declared martial law, the Solidarity Movement officially banned. Alina was jailed for over a year while Bogdan Borusewicz was forced into hiding. (In 1983 Alina and Bogdan secretly married, with Alina giving birth to a daughter the following summer and Bogdan attending the baptism disguised as an old woman.) Finally, in 1985, the communist government collapsed. Lech Walesa was elected president and Alina went back to working at the yard. Of her return, Alina said, "Here in the ship- yard I stopped being afraid, stopped running away, and became a real person." She died of cancer ten years later, at the age of 50. I considered then our own situation, our strike and Teddy and the rest. I saw myself with Tee, and Katima now, thought of Alina and Bogdan not so long ago, the brevity of it all and how time passes.

———

June ran on and our strike continued, the tension in the capital a spring trap noose. "This is not a campaign which will be lifted by the people or defeated by Teddy," Abel Dureci, a retired shop foreman said to me one night, "but rather a move- ment that will simply languish." Every day I made my rounds, attended meetings and spoke with people about the strike. Students from the University came to see me, boys like Daniel Osbera, Cris Con- tamorre and Bo Ratise who I knew casually before, appeared in my yard almost nightly now. Eager to talk, they impressed me with their knowledge, took turns discussing history: Pinochet and Allende, Kissinger and Nixon, Ireland's Sinn Fein rebellion of 1919 - the same year Gandhi introduced passive resistance to India - the sacking of Constantinople, the French and American and Chinese Revolutions, the battles in Davao City, the Boxer Rebellion, the massacre of Mexican students in Tlatelolco and Chinese dissidents in Tiananmen Square.

Two and three times a week I phoned the American Embassy, hoping the American Consul would agree to help us mediate with Teddy. I was told always that Erik Dukette was indisposed, until finally at the end of June, I received a call inviting me downtown. I arrived at the Embassy just after 10:00 a.m. and was brought upstairs to an office cluttered with files and books, folders and maps scattered about. The American Consul was square framed, with limp strands of red hair cut in uneven patches. His shoulders were flat, his round legs bending stiff. He called my name as if we were the best of long lost friends, waved at me to, "Come in, come in!" and extended his hand.

A stack of papers was removed from a leather chair and I was motioned to sit down. Dukette leaned against the front of his desk. "Can I get you something? A sandwich perhaps? You must be starved," he tapped his belly. "Better yet, I have some nice Texas steaks, freshly frozen and shipped. You should take a box home."

"No, thank you," I felt something sharp poke against my hip from between the leather cushions. "I'm fine."

"You're sure?" He signalled his secretary to close the door. "A cigarette then," he rattled off a list of brands. "We have Winstons, Kools. American tobacco. Raleighs in the hard box. Do you smoke?"

"No."

"Take them for your friends then. I have connections," he gave a wink while I reached behind me and removed a pen from beneath the chair's rear cushion. "Yes, well," The American

66

Consul shifted his feet on the floor, raised his eyebrows and said, "I'm glad you're here. It's good we can finally talk." He bent his fingers until the knuckles cracked then touched his forehead as if he'd forgotten something and offered me a drink. "A bit early for a sip, but a bottle perhaps? Something to take with you? A nice California wine? Anything you want. Gallo, Crane Lake, Ramey Hudson, Canyon Road?"

"No, really."

"Beer?"

"No."

"Bud? Coors? Schlitz malt liquor? Some candy then? Something sweet. American chocolates. Hershey, Pennsylvania. Take a box home for your lady friend."

The reference to Katima made me uncomfortable, and handing Dukette his pen, I decided to move things along and said, "About the strike."

"Of course," the American Consul stared at me, reached and pulled a brown leaf from the potted plant set atop the piles of folders on his desk. The office was surrounded by framed photographs of past American presidents, of Teddy with the American Consul, Teddy with the American singer Jessica Simpson, Teddy in uniform on stage at the Bameritan Bijou Theater. "It's all a misunderstanding really," he became suddenly serious. "It's gone on long enough, don't you think? What you want to achieve, what the General wants to achieve, is it all so different?"

I answered honestly, a bit uneasily, told him "It's very different, yes." From there, I went ahead and asked Dukette for his help in arbitrating our dispute with Teddy.

"You know, I'm sure, the General's arranged for an American director to visit Bamerita," he said this as if not hearing my request at all, and letting go of the leaf, he placed his hands behind him and breathed out through the flat of his turtle nose. "It's a bit embarrassing to find things as they are now, what with the General eager to make an impression and your strike leaving him with nothing to film."

"I'm sorry," I told him. "We're looking forward to sitting down and working things out in negotiation."

"You misunderstand," Dukette ran a finger back and forth above his left eye. "The General's not interested in negotiating. This is, how shall I say, a courtesy. The General is giving you notice of his plans to film. That's why you're here now. Filming will go back to the way it was before."

"But our strike won't allow."

"Be that as it may," the American Consul leaned forward and touched my knee. "Your strike, I'm afraid, exists only because the General has not yet attempted to end it."

I got up and went to stand behind the chair. Dukette gave me a moment, then smiled and said, "You have to know. If you're waiting for concessions, the General has no need. Why should he negotiate? Your strike is like hyenas trying to starve the lion. At the end of the day who suffers worst?" He shifted back, avuncular, and asked me next, "Why make things hard on yourself? Tell me what you want. We're both reasonable men. Let's deal in reality here. I'm in a position to get you anything. This is the way things are done. How's that old car of yours running? Have you seen the new Fords? Built like a rock. I can get you one, if you like. Riding a bike is no way for a man your age to travel." He made an effort to sit atop his desk, tried to hop high enough on his stiff legs but failed. "What about gas?" he slid down and stood again. "Do you need any? We have reserves you know. If there's something you want for your children, tell me. You're in a position to make a real difference here. All you have to do is say the word. This strike of yours can't go on. You won't win. If you came here thinking I might help you, that America might," he shook his head. "Business is politics and politics is business. I'm sure you understand. A bird in the hand," he said of Teddy. "The devil you know," he winked again. "Cut your loses. Give up the strike. Cooperate. Come on now, André, let me get you a sandwich. These opportunities aren't going to last forever. Once your strike is over, all your leverage will be gone."

I lifted my hands from the back of the chair, smoothed down my sleeves and thanked Dukette for his time. The American Consul sighed as if our conversation exhausted him. He followed after me as I got ready to leave, his fingers gripping my arm. "It isn't that we don't know who the General is," he said, "it's that none of it matters. If you want my advice, I would tell you again to abandon the strike."

"This is your expert opinion?"

"Sound counsel."

"As a neutral party?"

"No," he removed his hand, paused a moment before titling his head to the side and opening the door.

CHAPTER 5

L eo Covings lay in the large feather bed, inside the Rudy Vali Suite at the Bameritan Hyatt, looking nothing like the famous man Teddy Lamb had so gladly brought to Bamerita. At nine in the morning, he was only half awake and would have slept well past noon if the phone hadn't rung twice already and disturbed him. Each time, the soldier manning the front desk - the regular hotel staff being still on strike - informed Leo that he was due for brunch and an afternoon of filming. "Fine, yes, right." Leo used the heel of his hand to rub at his eyes, thought briefly of making an excuse and skipping the morning altogether, but knowing he was being paid a good sum of money, he hung down the phone and reached for his cigarettes on the nightstand.

From across the room he could see his reflection in the dresser mirror. His face had aged awkwardly, with lines and creases in places he could not have imagined just a few years ago.

He cleared his throat, flicked his lighter and set his feet on the floor. His head ached from overdrinking. He tugged the sheet back onto his knees, and as an exercise, tested his memory by trying to recall as many details as he could from last night.

Even before he arrived, the American Consul had sent several cartons of Camel cigarettes, six bottles of Kentucky whiskey, four containers of sun screen and a large box of Hershey chocolates to Leo's room. A quick survey of the floor found three of the bottles empty. Leo finished his cigarette, moved his toes through the carpet, worked his way toward getting dressed. Today Teddy planned on filming by the sea and Leo promised himself not to lose patience. Eleven years after his masterpiece - 'Portello's Confession' - he'd done little more than dabble at directing. Lacking the nerve to compete against himself, he'd lived well for some time off his reputation. "Old birds don't fly as high," Leo convinced himself. As long as studios were willing to pay him to serve as an advisor on their films, and colleges, conferences and conventions compensated him for speaking, he couldn't complain. He accepted the course of his career, was philosophical about his place in the pantheon, gave no further thought toward reconnecting, and then came the call from Teddy.

He sat on the edge of the bed and waited to get his bearings. For several minutes he debated a sip from the hair of the dog but didn't feel as yet like moving. What fascinated him initially about Teddy's film was the idea of turning an entire country into a movieland adventure. Teddy had pitched an idea to shoot a scene where all of Bamerita was dressed in coordinated costumes and gathered along the main roads, walking clockwise - perhaps dancing, perhaps singing - the footage recorded from overhead, creating the largest choreographed sequence ever captured on film. The vagueness of the story notwithstanding, Leo was intrigued enough to make the trip, then frustrated once he arrived as he could not get a handle on what Teddy was doing.

The scenes already filmed - several thousand hours worth - were a meandering montage, loosely narrated and unrelated. "I don't know what you're hoping to accomplish," Leo said after a fifth day of shooting, "but I suggest you take a look around." He referred then to the strike, encouraged the General to, "Work with what you have. Here's your story. Here's your drama. You can build a whole movie out of what's taking place on your streets right now and not bother with all this other heehaw."

Teddy disagreed. "With all due respect, what you see on the streets isn't drama. It's dirty dishwater and will be washed away tomorrow. This strike is nothing. We will not film it." He puffed out his narrow chest covered in colorful medals, and insisted again, "We will ignore it."

Leo changed his undershorts, pulled on a fresh pair of slacks, brushed his teeth and combed his hair. He smoked a second cigarette while looking for his shoes. Suddenly hungry, he decided to say nothing more about the film, to finish his commitment and be done. If the General couldn't see what was right in front of his nose, "To hell with him." He slipped on his shirt, blew smoke toward the window, was in the process of scooping up his wallet from the dresser when the phone rang again and a woman named Casmola said she was calling from the lobby.

—

—

Emilo woke and rolled onto his hip, relieved his bladder into a bucket. On the opposite side of the bed was his old guitar, two graphite canes, a tray with crumbs from a lettuce and jam sandwich, some juice and pills Paul Bernarr brought over. The clock on the nightstand said 10:17 p.m. Emilo shifted, fixed his shorts and turned on his lamp. He slept in fits and starts, napping now at odd hours. His feet in white plaster casts rested on pillows, his bones set with screws constantly aching. He sat up, slid his legs off the side of the bed, settled them carefully away from the bucket.

The pounding in his feet intensified, the pain worse when he moved. He placed his hands behind him on the edge of the bed, dropped slowly onto the seat of his pants and scooted around the floor where he took two more pills. The scars on his face were pink, the stitches removed, the slits healed in knotted lumps against the darker shade of his skin. His eyelids sagged halfway, his lips unevenly mended, looked like bits of half-moist clay torn apart and pinched back together. He crawled like a sea crab out to the front room where he sat with his back against the chair.

A few hours earlier André came by with lettuce and bread, a banana and two baked potatoes. Emilo listened to the news about the American Consul, rubbed at his lips and said, "What did you expect? You're standing in shit and surprised when your clothes start to stink. Think about it." He asked André to empty the bucket, said of Dukette, "The man's an ass but pay attention to what he's telling you. Why should we wait for them to fuck us? We can do better. A couple old warriors like you and me. You rode this pony as far as she'll go, André, now let's get serious."

After André left, Emilo ate and slept. Out in the front room, he used the flat end of a screwdriver to pry up three wooden slats in the floor, removed the cardboard box with the ammonium nitrate and nitro cellulose, potassium nitrate, charcoal and sulfur and attached the wires to the travel clock, the battery and fuse running to the tube set inside. He waited until just after midnight, when Kart Jabber used his key to enter the apartment through the rear of the store.

———

Teddy Lamb lay beneath green-yellow sheets, naked and cozy as hot ham laid between buttered toast. "You Americans," he mocked. "Why is it you work all day and sleep all night? Where's the sense in that? A good nap is what you need. Don't you ever want to howl at the moon?"

The American Consul stood at the end of the bed, acknowledged the ribbing with a slight nod. "If you prefer I wait downstairs, General."

"No, no. You're my alarm. Punctual as always," he slipped his legs from beneath the sheets, pressed the remote for the television, then pulled on his socks and boots, stood and walked across the floor to the bathroom where he emptied his bladder in full view. Dukette turned to look at the TV screen which showed the daily rushes from the filming conducted a few hours ago at the sea. "Leo has a remarkable eye, don't you think?"

Teddy noted the colors and camera angles. On the screen some two dozen Bameritans, rounded up that morning and forced back into costumes, were wearing the clothes of fishermen, the women in long farm girl dresses, the style early 1900's. Dukette watched several of the men digging deep holes in the sand near the tide. Two men and a woman were then placed in the holes, buried up to their shoulders. As the water rolled in, the tide darkened the sands and covered their faces.

"It's pretty dramatic," Teddy moved to his dresser where he stepped into a fresh pair of undershorts.

The American Consul cleared his throat, watched the three heads disappear beneath the water, the camera shifting to a shot further out at sea, while in the background Dukette could hear an unedited Leo Covings shouting, "Cut! Cut! Cut!" before the film went dark.

Father Piote appeared in the door, a half-eaten corned beef sandwich in his left hand. Dukette continued to stare at the suddenly black TV while Father Piote went and whispered something in Teddy's ear. Teddy patted the priest on the shoulder, finished buttoning his uniform, adjusted his medals, rewound the video and began watching again. "Look at that, will you?" he pointed to the three heads in their holes screaming. "Amazing, isn't it. Tell me, Erik, what possibly is better than making movies?"

———

Kart Jabber lay with Kara atop the bed. Angeline was on the far side of the room, naked in the red-backed chair, smoking, her legs crossed and pumping at the knee like the handle to a well. In their different shapes, Kart saw them as opposite ends of a funhouse mirror; Angeline tall and thin, her hair so blond it appeared almost white, her features sharp as the angelfish her father named her for, while Kara was short and round, like dark dough set on a flat wood surface, ready and waiting to be kneaded. Hungry, Kart sat up and began to dress. Kara rolled over and also started rooting around for her clothes. "I'll go with you."

"No. I'll be back in twenty minutes." He hadn't slept since leaving Emilo's, but was restless and knew if he wanted to get out at all today he had to go early or wait again until dark. He found his pants and pulled on his socks. The girls' apartment was one large room, the furniture secondhand, a bed and chairs, six pastel cushions, a half moon table and cedar trunk. Kart used his connections to get them bread and fruit, eggs and cheese. Unable to go to his place anymore, or to his parents, he shared the girls' bed, the arrangement creating a trinity of possibilities.

He left the apartment watching for soldiers, headed toward Weivre Avenue where Avus Keerl kept his truck. The last blast had taken out power lines near the capital's main police station. Kart walked now in the opposite direction, remembered the one time he agreed to take Angeline with him as he set a charge outside the Ministry of Transport. Angeline clung to his arm the whole way, dancing with the same anticipation and release as when her body shook beneath him during sex. Later, the scent of the bomb mixed on his skin with Angeline's own smell, his arms beneath hers, his hands sliding up to the front of her shoulders from behind. He could barely bring himself to touch Kara at all that night, had kept his head buried inside the ridge of Angeline's hip and against her back, trying not to show too much of how he was feeling. He laughed at this later, the way he felt and how soon enough he changed his mind and was completely in love with Kara.

The sun was just coming up, the color of ocher, the streets empty as he hurried back to the apartment with eggs and bread. He was thinking about the strike, how he needed to get his parents and the girls out of the capital before things collapsed and the fighting started. Once Teddy was gone and the war won he'd open a place of his own, a club where all his friends could come and drink and eat and Kara and Angeline would be his partners. They'd live together in a house he'd build and carry on the same as now, and if one of them should fall in love with someone else and wish to marry that would be fine, as there would be room for all and their children. This he thought while coming back, approaching the rear of the apartment, looking between the buildings a second before the soldiers pulled up in front and stormed inside. Two blackbirds cawed from overhead and flew toward the rooftops. Kara and Angeline shouted and tried getting away but the soldiers were too strong and wouldn't let them.

—

Ali and Feona lay on an old cloth tarp folded over in the center of the gym. With the strike in its second month and the schools closed for summer, the hallways and classrooms of All Kings smelled of soiled clothes, vegetables and smoke, sand and loam and trash gone sour. Windows were left open, the warm breeze through poplar branches mixing the scents together. Still dark, the children sleeping nearby filled the gym with sounds of hushed and shallow breathing, snores and sighs, the occasional soft whimpers and whisperings. Ali dressed and went outside to check on the day's water. Feona came barefoot a few minutes later, in khaki slacks and black t-shirt, her hair tied away from her face with a strip of yellow cloth.

"Phenom," Ali tried as always first thing in the morning to sound upbeat. "How did you sleep?"

"Alright," she touched her neck.

"Me, too. Like a rock," he reached out. "I woke up hard."

Feona pretended to be shocked and pulled away. They laughed at this, held their smiles as long as they could. For a week now they'd heard rumors about the strike losing ground. Friends spoke nervously of how it was but a matter of time before everything fell apart. The threat of the capital dissolving into violence, of Teddy sending soldiers into All Kings and ambushing the children as they gathered at the school forced Ali and Feona to begin making other plans.

Together they carried the water stored in several containers back into the cafeteria, the regular taps shut off by Teddy for some time. Three large pots were filled and placed on the stove to boil. The gas was also disconnected. Ali rigged propane tanks through the burners and started a flame. Sacks of oats and smaller bags of powdered eggs were bought and stored in the rear of the cafeteria. An open bag of oats was dragged into the cooking area and left beside the stove until the water boiled. Feona set out what bowls and spoons they had for serving, while the first of the children woke and headed outside to pee. Ali thought about the things he had to do that afternoon, the prospects and possibilities, and as Feona seemed to be thinking the same, he told her, "Not to worry, it's going to work. It will all be fine."

One of the younger boys in sandals too large, a blue t-shirt torn near the collar, with ginger dun skin and eyes wide and black, stopped in the doorway to the cafeteria and called out, "Waffles and syrup?"

Ali smiled and answered, "With whipped butter and fresh orange juice, Teo." The boy laughed and ran off. Ali glanced again at Feona, then back toward the cooking area. The sounds of others came from the gym, the water in the large pots starting to boil, the air already warm and filling with a harvest of steam.

———

In bed the Chief Inspector had bad dreams each time he dozed. He drank coffee in his office, sat heavy in the chair behind his desk while Everett Doyle paced impatiently about. As the Minister for Internal Planning, Doyle spoke with the Chief Inspector daily now, demanding updates on the strike and rebels in the hills, comparing notes and strategies. "About these rumors?" he asked.

"Talk is all," the Chief Inspector refilled his cup. His office was panelled in old wood, nicks and knots darkly stained, a few random plaques hung on silver nails. "There's always someone saying something," he shifted back in his chair. "I've heard a dozen rumors today already."

"All of which might be true."

"Take your pick," the Chief Inspector yawned. "Each is as good as the next."

"And yesterday?"

"The bombings have nothing to do with the strike."

"Don't be ridiculous," Doyle came toward the desk. "It's all the same. All NBDF. Nothing But Dumb Fucks. We should arrest every last one of them."

Warez set his coffee down and rubbed his face. "We're exploring our options. We've arrested plenty."

"What about those in the hills?"

"I'm a policeman, Everett. Insurgency I leave to the General."

"It's all insurgency," Doyle resumed pacing. He had nervous hands, even when stuffed into his pockets his fingers managed to crawl out. He went to the window and glanced down at the street, calculated once more the money lost each day during the strike. "We have to do something." His pug dog face stretched north and south. He turned to Warez and asked again, "What are they up to really? If you have information, Franco. If you know what's going to happen."

The Chief Inspector held up his hands, too tired to laugh. The whole of what there was continued to expand. He shifted his body deeper in his chair and on squeaky hinges answered, "Christ, Doyle, this is Bamerita. If you haven't figured out by now what's going to happen, my telling you isn't going to help."

CHAPTER 6

By mid-summer nearly all of our foods and fuels and daily staples were gone. If our strike had legs, they were wobbly now. I had to shave my head with old razors, the hairs cut back, pulling and snagged at the root. Katima would lather my scalp with the nub of soaps, would work the razor around as if guiding the blade of a damaged plow over rough fields. "There," she said each time she finished, kissed my head and patted me down with a towel. Not once did she suggest I simply let my hair grow out, understanding why I couldn't, as foolish as it seemed, the way it would look to others and what it would mean to me.

Soon more cracks in our solidarity appeared. Teddy's dealings with America, the loans he took, his sale of our businesses and natural resources, our farmlands and mineral deposits and exportation of Bamatine, our bottled water drawn from the sea, gave him leverage when he asked the States to assist in putting our movement down. We heard rumors of American soldiers being sent in, of troops coming to protect western interests, and rebels in the hills being ready to fight. The hardship of our strike lead to much second guessing. I rode my bike around the capital, offered encouragement and answered questions as best I could. As part of my pitch, I told people what Gandhi said of his own efforts to mount peaceful resistance, first in Newcastle and then in Champaran and Ahmedabad, how those committed must be willing to endure unconditionally until the very end. I did not tell them what else Gandhi said, how "Those who can not summon courage enough to take this line of action should return to work." This they seemed to figure out on their own.

In July, a handful of stores, small groceries and restaurants broke ranks and reopened for business. Those loyal to our strike threw bricks at their windows, while others came and bought meat and sugar, new shoes, tobacco and toilet paper. Teddy sent his soldiers in to protect the shops, had their shelves restocked with imported foods and goods, promised additional provisions to families who also quit the strike.

Discouraged, I thought of what else I could do, considered fasting to rally support, though I doubted people would care about me starving when they were hungry themselves. Such enterprise was likely to be construed as desperate, and what if by chance my fast caused friends to panic and resort to violence? How foolish would I feel then, as Gandhi regretted most when his passive protests lead to bloodshed in Delhi and Bombay, in Ahmedabad and worse, as Don Pendar noted, in Jallianwalla Bagh.

I returned home early one evening and found Don Pendar waiting for me in my front yard. "This

is for you," he handed me a newspaper clipping.
"For posting," he pointed up at my tower. We'd
spoken little since the start of the strike, both of
us busy with different concerns. The article he
gave me described a recent rebel attack in Columbia
where the National Liberation Army had coordinated a large offensive, killing nine soldiers
in an ambush along the Panamanian border in
Choco Province. I folded the clipping and put
it in my shirt pocket. The shadow from my tower
fell between us as I wiped my forehead and offered
Don Pendar a glass of water. "We've bottled a few
gallons. Come inside."

"No, thank you," he stepped further into the
shade and out of the sun. "If you don't mind, we
can talk here." His clothes were rumpled, his hair
brushed by fingers, his skin creased with dust. He
looked thinner, standing there with his shoulders
held back and eyes wide.

"Alright," I took off my sunglasses.

Don Pendar said, "About the strike. We've
all been patient, André."

"Patience is good."

"It isn't working."

"A few rough patches, nothing we can't fix."

"Enough is enough."

"In another week or so."

"Things will only be worse," he walked toward
the edge of my yard, glanced down the street then
came over to me again. "All of this," he bent forward
as if to make himself heard more clearly. "We need
you to call it off. People will listen if you tell them.
At tonight's meeting," he said.

"Seriously now," the idea was out of the question. I took a half step back and began countering
Don Pendar's request with a more positive review

of our strike. He refused to listen. I stopped talking, suspicious then, and holding my arms to the sides asked, "What exactly are you up to? What's going on?"

After he told me, I put my hat back on, pushed my sunglasses up over the bridge of my nose and replied as calmly as possible. "This is what you've come up with? This is what you want me to call the strike off for? I won't do it." The sun found my neck above the collar of my shirt. As I turned, my shadow shot out sideways as if it, too, were eager to escape. I excused myself, moved toward my house, said "There's nothing for us to discuss. Did you honestly think I'd agree to help you with such a ridiculous plan?"

———

I went inside and turned on the tap in the kitchen, clearing the air from the pipes. The water was not restored, though the electricity was back on. Upstairs I used a basin full of water saved in the tub to wash my face and hands, then stood for several seconds with my face in a towel, before dumping the dirty water into the toilet and returning downstairs.

Katima came in as I was resetting the electric clock in the kitchen. She had eggs, oranges and two tomatoes for our dinner. I turned around and found her dressed in a bar maid's costume, complete with busk and boned corset, a white chemise and blouse with puffed shoulders and neckline dropped to expose half her breasts. A red and green velour overvest was laced across her middle, her skirt cut above the knee, her high black boots with sharp stiletto heels surrounding shin and calf.

"What's this?" I stared, hoping there was a simple explanation.

"You like?" Katima in front of the counter, put her hands above her head and did a pirouette high up on her toes. "These nice soldiers gave it to me."

I tried not to panic, asked only, "When are you scheduled?"

"Tomorrow."

"And you're wearing it now?"

"I thought you might like to see. We may as well get some use out of it."

"But you can't," I shook my head. "It isn't safe."

"Safe or not, I won't go because we're on strike," Katima came and squeezed my fingers, twirled once more in her costume then went to the counter, wiped down the cutting board and began slicing the tomatoes. "It's ok," she said. "Teddy will make sure enough people show. He won't miss me."

I set our plates on the kitchen table while Katima mixed the eggs and tomatoes in a large green bowl, and worried still, I said, "He'll know you weren't there. He keeps track of these things."

Katima reached for the cooking oil, said what I already knew. "Teddy doesn't need my name on a list to do whatever he wants." She'd cut her hair short, the sun and salt waters having lightened the color, producing flecks of orange and streaks of sandy roan. With all the pools closed, she swam in the sea, out just beyond the first breaks and back. Her healthier clients joined her on the beach where Katima exercised them in the shallow roll of waves, coaching them without charge in deference to our strike. I went with her at night sometimes, after our meal, taking our bikes back into the capital as Katima stopped and checked on house-bound patients and families she knew were having a rough go.

All the gas in our neighborhood remained off and we relied on the small propane tank Ali brought over. I lit the line he showed me how to run through the stove's top burner. Katima warmed the oil and cooked the eggs with bits of fried potato saved from yesterday's meal. Once the eggs and potatoes were done, the bread placed on the sides of the pan and lightly toasted, we sat at the table and ate. Instead of discussing how Teddy had resumed filming with people pulled from their homes, how the American director brought in remained a mystery, and whether American soldiers might soon arrive, we tried other topics, spoke of Anita in the States safe from harm and how glad I was for this. I finished my eggs, moved my plate to the side and reached for Katima's hands.

I wanted to tell her about Don Pendar, the way he and others got it in their heads to seize the main warehouse and parts of the Port in order to kick start another revolution, but I hesitated. The redundancy of all that was happening felt overwhelming. I thought of myself twenty years ago and here again now, such an old rebel and widower, a one time agitator, no longer fearless and newly in love, a father pale and wanting, worried and wondering what to do. "I love you, you know?" I said, not for the first time but differently here. Katima across the table, tipped her head, put down her fork and asked, "André, what's wrong?"

Ten minutes later I was outside, in the heat of the evening, peddling north on my bike. I passed Roland Avenue, used my key to unlock Emilo's door, carried the leftover fried potatoes wrapped in foil, an orange and half a tomato. Emilo was in the front room, his canes beside the chair, his casted feet resting out in front of him, the bottoms black and flat from being dragged along the floor. I put the potatoes on a plate and began searching for a clean fork. "Pour me a drink, will you?" Emilo's voice was raspy, the air inside the apartment stale, the front window closed.

I brought his food, checked the whiskey left in the bottle he paid one of the neighbor boys to deliver. "There are ways to keep lubricated even during a strike," Emilo boasted, his mouth seeming to move in three different directions as his lips stretched and curled.

"Under the circumstances, I expected you to be drinking Port."

Emilo gave a crooked grin. "Pendar?"

"Just now," I handed him the glass, opened the window, let in fresh air.

He put the plate with potato in his lap. "You shouldn't be surprised. From day one, it's always been a matter of time."

I didn't agree and told him so. "The only thing inevitable is what will happen if we start a war. It's crazy," I said of Don Pendar's plan. "None of it will work."

"And still," Emilo held up a piece of potato on the end of his fork. "Logs on the fire, André. You can't stop what's set to burn."

———

87

I left Emilo's and rode across Unamuno Boulevard, where soldiers stopped me twice at checkpoints. My ID was reviewed against a list of names kept on a clipboard, the time of my arrival recorded, my destination demanded and written down as well. Halfway up Chetlan Avenue I passed Aaron Pemu's bookstore, the windows shaded and the front door padlocked. Aaron had opened his store shortly after the War of the Winds, had done well with his business until Teddy overthrew Dupala and began marking texts for censure: copies of Gunter Grass, Mark Twain, Vonnegut and Marlraux, Salman Rushdie and Italo Calvino. Aaron cleared his shelves of all such works, turned banned copies over to the soldiers who came to inspect his shop, built secret shelves behind his basement wall to stash additional copies for reading and resale. Three days before our strike began Aaron's store was raided, a dozen newly smuggled copies of Gabriel Garcia Marquez' *One Hundred Years Of Solitude* found hidden among the other books. Aaron was arrested and sent to Moulane Prison where we failed in our effort to get him out.

I rode around the far side of the University toward All Kings, which was built in the flat between two slopes a half mile away. In climbing the first hill, I struggled near the top, got off my bike and walked. The view from the crest overlooked Crasilia Park just east of All Kings. Statues done in bronze and stone and blackened iron were set along the footpaths, images of past leaders, larger-than-life casts of deposed presidents Jaope, Alsenda, Kenefie and Dupala, Jai Datisa and King Polanay. The most enormous of all was a silver and steel likeness of Teddy in full military vestment placed in the center of the Park, in a clearing where people took their dogs to piss.

I came down the hill, left my bike at the front of All Kings and went inside to find Ali. The building smelled of boiled cabbage and wet shoes. Ali and Feona were in the cafeteria serving watery soup and small slices of fruit to a hundred or more children crowded about. I kissed Feona, then asked Ali if he could take a short break. We walked down to one of the empty classrooms where Ali stood by the window, the last of the day's sunlight glowing through. "You look thin," I said.

"And you."

"But on me it looks good," I patted where the soft roll of my stomach used to be.

Ali asked about Katima. I removed my hat and placed it down on the nearest desk. From the hallway the sound of children laughing reached us, followed by several young boys running. "Listen," I cleared my throat and told him my news.

Ali shifted back from the window, the sharpness of his features illuminated. As a child, when troubled, he had a way of drawing his mouth in tight and hollowing his cheeks. He did this then, telling me as I finished, as if he had somehow heard my conversation with Emilo, "I'm not surprised. About all this," his voice went flat, then rallied a bit, as if trying to find it's rhythm. "Feona and I have been thinking. Whatever happens we're making arrangements."

I didn't understand. "What arrangements?"

Ali pointed toward the hall. "There are too many kids here now. We can't keep track of everyone. Some of the boys have gone missing. The soldiers are crazy. We don't have enough food. Feona and I want to move as many kids as we can before it's too late."

"Wait. Slow down." Again I said, "I don't understand. What do you mean move them?"

Ali went to the board at the front of the room and found a small piece of white chalk. "We've lined up a boat to get us past the patrols, out beyond Kaprischo Point and through the Straits," he drew the corresponding references. "If we can get some of the kids to the coast."

"You want to move them through the Straits?"

"That's right."

"And then what?"

"A group I've been in touch with will help them resettle."

"What group? Who's boat? Where exactly?" I walked between the desks toward Ali who promised as I came near, "It's doable." He set the chalk back and returned to the window. "If we can get even a few kids out of the country before things fall apart it will be worth it."

"But things aren't going to fall apart," I started in, then stopped myself, rolled my hands over and asked, "Who's boat is it?"

"Adeki Moore's uncle."

Adeki was a friend of Ali's, though the uncle I didn't know. "And he's willing to help?"

"He's being paid."

"I see," I used the chalk to draw a dollar sign on the board. "And the Straits? And the patrols? How familiar is your captain with them? Has he navigated these waters before, now that Teddy has cut everything off? Do you have the necessary information or are you just leaving things to chance?"

The sun outside had slipped behind the hill, its glow fainter. I approached the window while Ali addressed my concerns with, "It's the best plan we could come up with."

"That may be true, but this alone doesn't make it a good one." I thought once more of Don Pendar, and worried again about all the worst that could happen, I asked, "If you do manage to fill your boat and navigate the waters, will you and Feona stay overseas with the children?"

"No," Ali shoved his hands deep into his pockets, his arms thin and long. "I'll go and come back." His lips and cheeks became drawn again as he changed the subject. "About the money. We don't have enough."

I hesitated before asking, "How much does your captain want?"

"Five thousand."

"Bulecra?"

"Dollars."

"Ali!" The amount was obscene. I expected this to be the end of things, but instead Ali said, "We've half of it."

"You've half? How?"

"Nickels and dimes. Friends and Anita," he told me of the money his sister raised in the States. I shook my head. "This plan of yours."

"Is all we have," his eyes held mine.

"Even if I could," I reminded him of the difficulty in exchanging bulecra to dollars, how just yesterday Teddy extended his freeze on foreign currency sales, the value of our national tender down 40% since the start of our strike. I reached for my hat, put it back on my head, then took it off again and returned it to the desk. "The children are safe now," I tried this, but Ali could tell even I didn't believe. "There must be something else you can do."

"We'll pay you back."

"That isn't what I'm saying. I don't care about that," I picked up my hat again, turned it over in my hand, set it on my head once more and felt in my pocket for my sunglasses. Ali in worn jeans, faded t-shirt and ancient sandals, his wheat-brown hair hanging across his forehead and brushed back from his eyes, waited for my final word. A new group of boys ran by in the hall, their laughter rising, their footsteps swift as they raced together along the yellowed tiles, moving as a single band of loose limbs and beautiful heads. As they passed the open door, each boy stole a quick peek inside, their faces brown and bright and innocent. I listened to the echo of their footsteps, and as they faded, placed my hands on each side of Ali's shoulders. "Give me a day to see what I can do." I looked out the window, at the darkening sky, pictured a boat in the waters off Kaprischo Point, navigating through the flat black surface of unlit channels, the night sea parted by the fullness of the moon.

———

I found my bike where I left it and rode back across Unamuno Boulevard. My father was reading on his front porch when I arrived, seated beneath a white light, the arms and back of his wicker chair curved around him, his large frame aglow. I bent to roll down the rubberbands from my pant cuffs, then stretched the knots in my back. "All that peddling will keep you fit and trim like me," my father closed his book as I came up the steps. I rubbed at my neck, apologized for being late. "I went to see Ali."

"How's the boy?"

"He's alright. A bit thin. And tired."

"It's a lot he's taken on."

"Too much, I think."

"He's stubborn like his mother." The reference to Tamina, while not unusual, seemed more deliberate then and caused me to ask, "When was the last time you spoke with Ali?"

"Yesterday. He wanted some advice."

"About Kaprischo Point?"

"He was concerned about your reaction."

I sat down on the top step, my back still tight and my legs extended. "What did you tell him?"

"I said I'd make a few calls. It can't hurt to have more information. Still the boy is right, stay or go, these kids are in the soup." My father moved his hands from the center of his stomach, and setting his book - a dogeared copy of *One Hundred Years Of Solitude* - beneath his chair, held out his arm for me to help him up.

His car was an old Fiat sedan, the roof high and rounded. As he had trouble driving now, I took him where he needed to go, his key kept on the ring with my own. We headed out, watching for soldiers assigned to follow us, circled the first few blocks, drove east then west with the headlights dimmed before resuming a normal course. Our meeting was in the sub-basement of the hospital on the south end of the capital, and cutting back across the numbered streets I spoke with my father about Don Pendar and what I should do tonight.

"They've given the strike a good amount of time, André."

"It isn't enough."

"And yet what more is there to expect?"

"Their idea's apocalyptic."

"Possibly so," my father cracked his window for fresh air. "Still, they won't listen now if you object. The situation is this. If you try tonight for something different they'll shout you down," he tapped the dashboard. "Harsh truths, André. We can't afford to be divided. If there are flaws in their plan, we must fix them," he reached across the front seat of the car and squeezed my arm. "Do you understand?"

Halfway to the hospital, all the traffic lights went black, forcing me to slow at each intersection and look from side to side. We avoided the checkpoints, arrived at the hospital sometime after 9:00 p.m. and drove down the ramp at the east end of the parking lot. I shut off the car, shifted on the front seat in order to face my father. I was about to argue that seizing the Port was irresponsible and starting a war worse, was eager to tell the others exactly this, to speak of our children, of history and all those we buried and would bury in the weeks to come if we did as Don Pendar planned, but then I noticed a man in a tan coat and dark slacks coming from the hospital and approaching his car.

The man went to his driver's side door and inserted the key he held in his hand. For whatever reason the key didn't work. The lock stuck and refused to turn as the man twisted his wrist first left then right then left again. He pulled the key out, stared at it a moment, felt the lock with his fingers, reinserted the key, twisted this time more vigorously, jiggling his whole arm up and down. Frustrated, he snatched out the key, yanked on the handle, slapped the window, struck the roof with his fist, tossed up his arms, cursed and smacked the door again. Only after all of this did it occur to him to try the lock on the passenger side of the car. He went around, reinserted the key, clicked open the lock, slid inside behind the wheel and drove off.

I got out and went to help my father from the car. We walked slowly through the parking lot and down the stairs into the basement where the men already gathered called our names and let us pass up to the front of the room. I stopped and turned back to face them, waited an extra moment until the room was completely quiet then said, "Alright. Alright," and told everyone what they wanted to hear.

CHAPTER 7

H is first night in the capital, Colonel Pashfeld was invited to dinner by Teddy Lamb. Eager to curry favor with the American, Teddy served southern fried chicken and beer brewed fresh in cold mountain streams. "A General's uniform?" Doug Pashfeld touched his own row of red and blue medals, said to Erik Dukette the next morning. "What is it with these guys?"

The American Consul went to his window while the Colonel settled back in his chair. Each day now Colonel Pashfeld came and spoke with the American Consul, hoping to get a better fix on the situation. He sat and listened, rubbed his chin, crossed and uncrossed his legs, posed many questions. He chafed at what had became of his career, his days as a military man winding down like this. "I'm no diplomat. I'm no statesman. What the hell am I doing here?" he asked the American Consul who wondered the same, stood and stared out the window at the American soldiers passing below.

———

The meeting at the hospital ran late and I didn't get home until after 2:00 a.m. Katima had fallen asleep with the lamp still on and a book by Wole Soyinka in her lap. I stroked her hair, studied in great detail the shape of her face, the curve of her cheek and how her mouth parted ever so slightly as if about to whisper some secret from her dreams. She woke and asked, "How did it go?"

I told her then what had happened, all of it from the beginning, leaving nothing out. Katima sat up, pushed the sheet away. I stood and slipped off my shoes, sat back on the bed, leaned in and brought her toward me.

———

After a few hours sleep I left the house and pedalled across town to Daniel Osbera's apartment. As a child, Daniel was friends with Anita, had spent time at our house and played games of tag and hide-and-seek around my tower. As a young man now, his treatment of my tower was more reflective, his studies at the University having shifted his interests, his curiosity for my industry and unconventional views. He came by my office, spent time in my yard, asked questions, explored history both personal and otherwise. Intrigued enough to listen when I spoke of Gandhi, he wondered where such sensibilities fit into the otherwise volatile vacuum that was Bamerita. A tall boy with loose arms and lanky rhythms, black hair worn as a shaggy dog, Daniel worked hard during our strike, he and his friends indispensable to our effort, and for this then I came early in the morning to disturb them.

The buildings near the University were half empty, the strike sending most students home to their families. I took the stairs to the third floor and knocked. Daniel's apartment was small, the front room cramped, a table and lamp for studying, stacks of books and clothing scattered over three chairs. The window to the left was raised several inches, though the air in the apartment was sour. Daniel let me in, half-asleep as he asked, "Has something happened?"

Riding over, I'd rehearsed what I was going to say. The plan I had in mind was not yet fully formed, and yet, as I could think of nothing else, my choices limited and no time to delay, I went and stood by the window, my hat in my left hand, the rubberbands around my pant legs rolled down. Daniel's roommates, Cris and Bo, came out and also asked, "What's up, Mr. Mafante?" Cris was fair-skinned and small, like an image in a Giovanni Segantini painting, while Bo was a large egg with deep cut muscles. I looked between the three, realized how young they were still, just boys, and how much I was counting on their support. I described the plot to seize the main warehouse, explained why I told the others that I would help and how, "If we're to stop them, it's important everyone trusts me first."

Daniel by the table, considered my claim then asked, "Stop them how?"

A pot of yesterday's coffee was reheated, the coils in the electric stove warmed by a battery Bo had rigged with copper wires. Cris handed me a mug which tasted bitter and settled poorly in my stomach. I answered Daniel's question, told them what I was thinking. "If we can fill the streets before the others make their move, they won't be able to attack the Port." I presented my idea for organizing a demonstration. "We'll put a march together, a rally to show solidarity for the strike."

"You want to block the Port so the others won't storm the warehouse?"

"That's right," I began to ramble, painted our effort as, "The perfect way to prove how united we are. Think about it," I said. "The reason we've failed to attract support from overseas is that the foreign press won't cover us. There's nothing sexy about a strike, but a demonstration is visual. A march is seductive, a rally something the media will want to show." I raised my coffee mug and nodded as if everything now made sense. "If we can get the world to observe us, Teddy will lose all clout. There are stations I know that will run our rally live once we set up a broadcast. I'm told it's possible to feed images through a computer and circumvent the normal airwaves so Teddy can't block our transmission."

"A webcam," Cris said.

"It's possible," Bo agreed.

I had their attention now, confirmed with Bo that we could send a live feed overseas to a station that would take our lead and dispatch it to others. I promised to make all arrangements, tried to sound confident and swore, "Teddy won't interfere as long as we're peaceful and the cameras are rolling. We have a few days to get organized. It's doable if we set ourselves to it."

Eventually everyone agreed. Cris grabbed a pad and pen and began plotting ways to contact people without Don Pendar and the others finding out. Bo focused on how best to manage our broadcast, while I worked with Daniel on coordinating the logistics of our march. An hour past before the rush of adrenaline gave way and Cris asked again, "About the soldiers? And Teddy? How long do you think they'll give us once we start?"

The concern was reasonable, though in trying to present the best response, I stumbled about for the right words, resorted to quoting Gandhi: "I believe non-violence infinitely superior to violence, forgiveness more manly than punishment." I defined Sadagraph for them as, "the firmness in a good cause," and quoted, too, what Theodore Roszak said about, "People try nonviolence for a week, and when it doesn't work, they go back to violence which hasn't worked for centuries." All of this seemed like so much rhetoric until Daniel took up the challenge and told his friends to, "Forget Teddy. Forget the soldiers. I mean think about it," he flicked his hands in the air. "We'll be on TV. What can they do to us, really? I mean really, come on."

———

I retrieved my bike from the lobby and headed back uptown. Daniel, Cris, Bo and I were to meet again at the apartment at 6:00 p.m. and review our progress, while Don Pendar and Mical Delmont were already waiting for me to go over plans from last night. The duality of my conspiracy made me dizzy. Between the strike, the demonstration and my deception regarding the Port, I worried about pulling everything off. On Appress Avenue, I pedalled north, parallel to the sea, when a small brown car appeared suddenly and cut me off. A man in street clothes got out on the passenger's side and grabbed my handlebars. "If you don't mind, Mr. Mafante, please."

My bike was placed atop the metal rack on the trunk of the car, while I was made to sit in the front seat beside the driver. A handgun lay in the space between us which the driver didn't try to conceal. The man in back had a black radio which cracked and buzzed at regular intervals. We left the city by side streets, avoiding all checkpoints, the men saying only enough to let me know where we were headed.

Outside the capital, Bamerita became quickly a stretch of flat farms, followed by forest and hills. Smaller towns, shops and factories sat back from the road. After twenty minutes we turned down a dirt path and stopped in front of an old wheat silo bleached beige by the sun. Two men came from behind the silo and approached the car as we got out. One of the new men slid behind the wheel and drove the car inside the silo while the rest of us hiked into the woods.

Twice the man with the radio ducked away, returning each time to nod at the others. We stopped finally after some thirty minutes, having reached a clearing where more men were waiting. Each man was well whiskered, wore dust stained clothes, their skin browned by weeks outdoors. Boxes of supplies, old rifles and silver cans were spread among the surrounding trees, the branches overhead bowed and weaved together, a network of ropes and boards laid out in the branches in an elaborate series of catwalks. The man who drove the car touched my shoulder and had me continue between the trees and down a short incline.

We wound around the hillside until the rocks presented the opening to a cave. A lantern glowed inside. Justin was there with his back to me, the lantern illuminating a small wooden table, a half dozen cardboard boxes and a small machine producing a low whir and a click-click-clicking sound. The machine was an old ink wheel mimeograph, silver-grey with a smooth metal carriage and a round plastic bottle of blue ink loaded into the underside. Several stacks of flyers were placed in boxes beneath the table. I raised my hand to check the height of the cave, my shadow stretching out in front of me as I let Justin know I was there.

When he turned, I thought at first the glow from the lantern was responsible for making his face look as it did. His coloring was yellow, his cheeks hollow, his whiskers white. Although we were the same age, and had known one another since before we fought in the War of the Winds, Justin now looked ancient, the sounds he made when he spoke raw and rasped. "It's good to see you, André," he coughed and bent forward. "I'm glad you're here. Come," he waved me toward the table, handed me the most recent flyer, a new essay condemning Teddy and calling for measures well beyond our strike. As I read, Justin tapped his chest and coughed again. Before I finished, he cupped my elbow and steered me back toward the mouth of the cave where we emerged squinting against the sunlight.

In the heat, Justin's stride was suspect. He didn't release my elbow until we'd reached the front of a large silver rock. The hillside provided a view of the trail below. I stood near the bluff overlooking the trees while Justin asked about my father.

"He's well."

"Good. I'm glad to hear. That's good for us," he massaged his throat, spat out grey phlegm, wiped his mouth with his sleeve. "And Emilo? How's he doing?"

"His feet seem to be healing."

"And his face?"

"Who can tell."

"Ha!" Justin drew in three short breaths as if stealing something from the air. He pressed two fingers against his chest, his mouth still open. I noticed his teeth had gone dark in patches near the gums, his lips cracked and white. "You need to see a doctor."

"I'm fine."

"No you're not."

"A touch of flu is all."

"You're jaundiced. You're too thin. You should come back to the city and let Bernarr have a look at you."

"Soon," Justin shifted further against the rock, mentioned the meeting at the hospital last night and how, "It's good what you did."

"You heard?"

"Word travels. It's why you're here. I'm glad you came around, André. And still, this plan of theirs," he said, surprising me. "It's not the first thing I would have chosen."

"No, it's not," I agreed at once, relieved Justin felt the same. "It's crazy."

"Fish in a barrel if they charge the Port on their own. The water cuts them off, traps them in. There are better ways."

"You're right," I spoke without wanting to think too far ahead, knowing Justin as I did. At Tamina's funeral, he stood beside me, clenching his fist, his faith unwavering even then. He celebrated the War of the Winds, maintained a firm conviction for revolution and saw no reason to alter his belief after Teddy's coup. I didn't expect a full conversion, and still I was encouraged to hear him say, "They haven't thought things through."

"No they haven't."

"This Pendar."

"He doesn't know."

"But you and I, André. We know, don't we? A couple of old warriors," he said just like Emilo. "We've been here before, haven't we? The more things change," he coughed, pushed his white hair back behind his ears, reminded me, "I've not been out in the woods all this time whittling and watching birds." He listed then specific efforts, plots to sabotage government holdings, the mines and movie and water plant, all the recent ambushes, the battles his men had with soldiers, raids to reclaim several hundred acres of farmland on the south-west side. "And now, as things are this close, we can't lose our heads."

It was true what Justin said. I looked back toward the bluff, told him, "We need to be patient. Here we are again, yes, but things have changed. This time we know better. We're not going to bumble and stumble and rely on luck."

"This time, you're right," Justin spat again and rubbed his throat. "That's why you're here. Who better to make things work than you and me? Why else do you suppose Pendar came to talk with each of us? He's smart enough to know his deficiencies, wise enough to understand we've been there before." The creases near Justin's left eye twitched. He bent over, his hands on his knees as he caught his breath, his white hair dangling like webs. After a moment he lifted his head, touched the side of his cheek with his index finger and waved me closer. "It's good, you know, you're being here. You hoped for something else, I understand, and that's ok. I don't blame you. In a perfect world, André. But she isn't, is she? This way together, we'll be sure to get things right. In the end, that's all that matters, no?"

We spent the next three hours discussing ways to improve Don Pendar's plan. Disappointed how quickly my high hopes vanished, I was tempted to confess last night was a mistake and that I never meant to help anyone start a revolution. Instead, Justin and I put together a new strategy, concentrated on mobilizing the men in the hills and making a move on the capital.

We decided to create a series of diversions, to go after the mines and the water plant again, the train tracks and travel routes with a handful of men setting explosives. The rest of Justin's men would approach the city from both sides of the highway, using the woods for cover. Positions would be established along the way, near the Port and roads leading to and from the capital. Once the men in the city drew soldiers to the main warehouse, the men from the hills would launch a coordinated counter attack, reinforcing the fight at the Port while taking on soldiers rushing back from the mines and waterworks. Everything was targeted to start in five days, as the men moved down from the hills, meaning the demonstration I was coordinating with Daniel and the others had to begin in less then 72 hours.

Justin and I returned to the open area where he slid his hand from my elbow and embraced me. "There it is then, André." I could feel his ribs beneath his shirt brittle as a bird cage. The same two men from earlier hiked with me through the woods, each of us carrying a stack of Justin's latest flyer. We drove to the capital without incident. I had missed my meeting with Don Pendar, was eager to see how Katima was doing and to speak with Daniel, Cris and Bo. The sun was white and high on my shoulders as I peddled off on my bike. Nervous, not wanting to think what the capital might look like by this time next week, I took Justin's flyers and set them in a single pile on the first bench I passed. Absent a stone to weigh them down, the papers flew in the breeze as I rode off. I saw them land where they wanted, the written words face down.

———

I went first to Davi's office at Suntu Husbandry and Farming Group, where Katima had spent the day avoiding the soldiers as she was otherwise scheduled to film. Neither Davi or Katima were there however, and winded, I rode back to the apartments near the University where Daniel, Cris and Bo were waiting.

Our strategy for spreading word about the demonstration involved the principles of a Ponzi scheme, where one person passed news to three friends who in turn sent word to three more and so on and so on. The need for discretion was explained, people instructed to deal only with acquaintances who could be trusted. The game was tricky, the process requiring a certain intuition. Daniel, Cris and Bo made progress, their enterprise offsetting my time away with Justin. Bo had found a webcam and a high speed computer, arranged to run the equipment from a fourth floor apartment near the main warehouse, while Daniel and Cris canvassed the capital for supporters. I left them with directions for the evening and we arranged to meet early the next day.

By 8:30 p.m. I'd picked up my father and driven to the strip mall across Yushco Street where Don Pendar and the others had gathered in the basement of the closed Piggly Wiggly. Upon learning of my conversation with Justin everyone cheered. The next stage of our plan came together quickly, and just after midnight I dropped my father back at his house and rode my bike home.

Katima was in the front room, the electricity off, the house lit by candles. I was relieved to find her there and hurried in wanting to know, "What happened today?" The shadows in the room made it hard for me to see the Chief Inspector sitting there as well. Halfway across the floor, I stopped and stared. Warez stood and greeted me. "There you are, André."

Katima had me come and sit beside her on the couch. "The Chief Inspector's promised to fix our lights," she squeezed my fingers hard. Warez in the chair across from us, removed a cell phone from inside his jacket pocket and dialed a number. A half minute later our lights were restored. "There then."

A buzzer on the stove started to ring. Katima blew out the candles, went into the kitchen. "Do you mind if I smoke?" the Chief Inspector sat down again, took a cigarette from his pocket, lit it with a match cupped in his palm. "I would have come earlier," he said, "but I knew you were out."

I refused the bait, replied "Is there something we can do for you, Franco?"

"A little talk."

"At this hour?"

"A few minutes," he looked for a place to flick his ash. I pointed to the bowl on the bookshelf and he went to retrieve it. "You're uncomfortable," he said as he returned to the chair.

"I don't know what you want."

"I didn't used to make you nervous."

"You worked for Dupala then. You work for Teddy now."

Warez puffed twice on his cigarette, his moustache hiding much of his upper lip. He shifted forward in his chair, his white slacks riding up and wrinkling across his thighs. "Perhaps you'd feel differently if I resigned my post and opened a spice and cheese shop in the city. But what good would I be to you then?"

Katima returned from the kitchen and sat back on the couch. "I'd offer you water but," she showed empty hands. I touched her arm. Warez lifted slightly from his chair as she entered, then sat and began again. "I was saying it's good I'm the Chief Inspector and not someone else. André hasn't been arrested, Gabriel and Ali are well, most of your friends are safe and not in jail despite the strike, and why do you suppose that is?" He gave us a second to consider, crushed his cigarette in the bowl, rubbed his hand across his moustache. The cuffs of his slacks fell across dark boots. "Your filming today," he continued looking at Katima. "Tell me, how did it go? Some confusion in your time before the camera. Bad luck no doubt, but these things happen."

Reference to the day's shoot caused me to lean forward on the couch. "It's my fault. The schedule wasn't clear," I began making excuses, calculating the penalty. Warez tapped my knee. "Let me see what I can do." He reached for his hat, made as if about to go then said, "Just one more thing. You've had a long day so I won't keep you but a few minutes more. Just a question."

"About?"

"The future," Warez said.

I moved closer to Katima. "I can't tell the future."

The Chief Inspector lit another cigarette, blew smoke through his teeth. "I understand your friend Justin isn't well."

"I wouldn't know about that."

"And yet you just saw him."

Katima laughed as if the possibility was absurd. I brought my hands together in front of my chest. "Now you're listening to rumors, Franco? You know the way these stories get started."

"They grow from the root," Warez drew fresh smoke and lowered his arm, let his cigarette dangle over his knee. He waited a moment then straightened suddenly, as if an idea had only just come to him. "If you'd rather deal with Teddy," he put his cigarette between his lips, pushed himself out of the chair with an audible, "Oooff," picked up his hat and started across the room.

I followed him out the front door and onto the porch where I asked, "About Katima?"

"Happy to help, if you'll help me," Warez flicked his cigarette toward the street. When I didn't reply he sighed as if disappointed in me. "How long have we known one another, André? Do you think I'd sell you short? Have I changed so much since Dupala?"

I treaded carefully, told him honestly, "It isn't so much a question of change. You're more adaptable. If not complete capitulation you're certainly a chameleon."

"Really? You think?" Warez touched his chin, scuffed his boots on the porch, turned away from me and pointed overhead. "Look," his finger was aimed at the sky dark and clouded over. "The moon is there. Can you see?"

"I know she's there."

"Because you've seen her before."

"I've seen her there and not there," I rested against the rail, knew what Warez was trying to say and told him again, "I can't tell you anything. You're asking too much."

"A bit of faith," he pushed back the brim of his hat, had me study his eyes which seemed more weary and restless than earlier. I remained silent. Warez resorted to mentioning Emilo, Don Pendar, Ali and my father. He spoke of Justin and how, "It's a shame he's sick, but then everyone's state of health is precarious these days. Who ever knows? One minute we're here and the next," he snapped his fingers.

I took the warning for what it was, shifted on the soles of my feet. Warez stepped toward me. We were the same height though the Chief Inspector had a habit of stretching his neck and lowering his chin as if gazing down. I studied his face, considered returning inside, of locking the door and taking my chances but the risk seemed ill-omened, and rubbing the ache from my lower back with the flat of my thumbs, asked again, "About Katima?"

"Not to worry."

"And Ali?"

"Of course."

"And my father and Emilo?"

"Your father," the Chief Inspector offered this.

"You have it all wrong," I told him then, correcting his reference to Justin, insisting "I went to the woods to make sure they stayed away. They have no plan," I said, creating another deception, diverting him from the hills back to the capital. The moon remained where she was, the sky above revealing nothing. "If you want to help," I started with this, explained what he needed to know. The Chief Inspector felt for his matches, walked with me down the steps. Satisfied he said, "Not to worry," crossed the curb and went back down the street to his car.

CHAPTER 8

Paul Bernarr wondered what to make of the news. He walked through the hospital, from the examination area back to his office, past the supply rooms mostly empty now as Teddy siphoned off the reserves, withheld medicines from the public as penalty for the strike. Earlier André and Davi had both left messages on the hospital line. Bernarr had tried calling them back but had not gotten through. His days were composed completely of improvisation, the way he treated patients with whatever instruments and medicines he managed to acquire from underground markets. Just before 6:00 p.m., he diagnosed a young woman with severe pain in her belly. "Diverticulitis. An intestinal infection."

"It hurts like crazy."

He decided to manage her condition with the antibiotics on hand. "Will I have to stay?" she asked.

"It would be best."

"I hate to miss," and here she mentioned the rally as she assumed the good doctor already knew.

He arranged for the woman to be made comfortable in the ward, then left the examination area and went back to his office. At the meeting last night, he was as surprised as anyone by André's decision. If, in the heat of the moment, he'd given André the benefit of the doubt, it had never made sense until now. "So this is what you've been up to," Dr. Bernarr shook his head, looked toward the window, imagined the possibilities, stopped and considered them again.

—

Leo Covings lay in bed with Casmola, wondering if there would be any unpleasantness here. The possibility was rife in situations like this, the expectation each woman he slept with had for being cast in his next film. Casmela came with headshots and an audition tape. She memorized details from Leo's career, recited them while touching his shoulder and then his knee. She laughed at his jokes, gave attentive replies to his comments. Seduced by the shimmy of her long black hair, he allowed her to kiss him as he spoke about Teddy's project. She pulled away afterward, feigning surprise. Caught up in the moment, she hesitated, waited for permission to kiss him again, pretending as he slipped a hand beneath her shirt that she didn't quite know what he was doing.

Leo rolled and reached for a cigarette, decided to give her five minutes more then ask her to leave. At his age there was no chance of rising to the possibility of seconds, and beyond this, he'd work he was anxious to get to now. The film he was brought in to help marshal through had, after many fits and false starts, finally taken a positive turn. He was excited and tried to concentrate in earnest, resented all other demands on his time; the daily interruptions by the American Consul, agents from the ministries, government journalists and representatives from the clergy. He was invited to dine with Teddy, to have drinks with Everett Doyle, all an increasing annoyance. He also had no desire to indulge Casmola and compromise his film by placating her with even the smallest part. He lay blowing smoke, not listening as she chattered on at him, measuring off the time before he finally said, "You should probably go,"

He got out of bed and walked to the bathroom, already plotting a new scene for the film. The vastness of the project, the promise and possibilities he could not quite get a handle on at first frustrated and then inspired him. He reviewed the rushes, went over old footage, searched for a thread to give the film its center. He put up a storyboard in his hotel room and tried to hammer out a script, yet nothing quite came together until yesterday, when André Mafante arrived and knocked on his door.

—

Emilo woke early and shuffled on casted feet. His head heavy from last night's whiskey and pills, he went into the bathroom and braced himself with hands flat against the wall, peeing a stream of something more than yellow. He blamed his dreams for waking him, but there was nothing he could remember. Turning, he looked back through the apartment toward the window, saw

shadows shift between the half parted drapes, rising
to the ceiling. A scratchy rhythm from the street
below, the sound of stones rubbing against leather.
He found his canes, went to the window and called
down, "What's going on?"

Last night, and the night before, as André
brought cheese and yams, Emilo pressed him to
come clean. "After all these years, don't think you
got me fooled. I know you're up to something."

"What possibly?" André raised his hands.
"I'm just dealing with the inevitable, like you
said."

"Are you now?" Emilo waved a stick of
cheese. "An epiphany, is that it? I don't think so.
Come on, André. It's me, Emilo. Give your old pal
the news."

He moved from the window toward the door,
his steps unsteady. He stumbled, righted himself,
and determined to get downstairs, went into the
kitchen where he searched the drawers for tools.
The cast on his right foot ran up to the middle of
his shin, the plaster thinner near the edge. He carried a screwdriver, pliers and hammer back into the
front room and sat near the window where he tore
away one small piece followed by another. The cast
was thicker around his ankle and across the top of
his foot. He applied the hammer and screwdriver,
tapped until a crack appeared, used the pliers to
separate the seam and split the seal.

Inside the bones had healed with bumps
buckling the skin. Emilo saw a pale paw covered
with flakes of moist and pasty flesh. He brushed
off the chalky white, moved his toes tentatively,
then repeated the process. His left foot was red
and gnarled, the toes oddly curved. He cleared the
plaster, placed his hands on the arms of the chair

and stood slowly. The tendon running from ball to heel had shrunk after so many weeks, and taking his first free step, a sharp pain sent Emilo crashing. "God fuck it!" He climbed to his knees, grabbed his canes and crossed them like swords before standing again, shifting his weight onto his heels and walking back to the bedroom where he sat and slipped on his pants, socks and boots. The support from his boots helped ease the pain in his feet. Still tender, he tested his stride, made his way down the stairs, through the store and to the street where more people were marching, men and women and children together. Emilo stood at the curb and called for André, was told he was already up ahead. He tapped the ground with his canes, rolled his eyes at the nonsense, the idea of a rally. How long could a demonstration like this last anyway? No more than a few hours. If no one lingered and the streets were cleared in a timely fashion, there was no need to worry. All the rest would go on as planned.

He adjusted his weight again, maneuvered against the pain in his feet, tried joining the march, but realizing he couldn't keep up, held out hope some straggler in a car would stop for him. Toward the corner his luck changed, a military jeep with three of Teddy's soldiers came quickly and insisted on giving Emilo a ride.

———

"Come, come," Teddy shouted from the water. "The sea is warm. Can you think of a better way to start your day than this?" Early still, not yet 6:00 a.m. and well before the time he typically crawled from bed, Teddy invited Doug Pashfeld,

Erik Dukette and a few lady friends to splash about with him in the water. Colonel Pashfeld arrived in uniform, his dark boots sunk in the sands, the white foam rolling against hard leather. "Look at you," Teddy laughed. "Where are your trunks? Why are you just standing there on this beautiful morning?"

Pashfeld stared back at the water. "If there's something you wish to talk about, General."

"Talk, talk, talk. Is that all you Americans can think of?" Teddy grabbed the nearest girl who squealed with false delight. "I invited you to swim," he slipped down and bobbed back up again. "After breakfast, if you still feel a need, we can talk then. Maybe we'll even have something to chat about later," he shoved the girl away and floated on his back.

Erik Dukette wore a baggy bathing suit, dark blue and pulled up beneath the underside of his belly. He entered the water hesitantly, forcing a smile while one of the girls came and took his hand, her breasts splashed with sea spray as she guided him further from shore. "Relax!" Teddy yelled, dunked his head and blew water from his mouth like a fountain. Doug Pashfeld studied the scene, observed the General, his instincts alerted, he tried gauging what didn't add up. When his cell phone rang he answered it, turned hurriedly and trotted back to his jeep. Teddy in waist high waters, stood and waved after the Colonel in mock surprise. "Why Douglas, what is it? What ever's the matter?"

———

The day before our demonstration, I went to All Kings and delivered the money I promised Ali. We stood outside, behind the school, near a stone grass field where several children ran about in a ragtag game of soccer. The remains of a well worn ball was wound tightly in grey tape and passed back and forth. I watched the children play, thought about the urgency of our days, and feeling then suddenly within the eye of the storm, said as much to Ali. "If we could keep just this," I told him.

I left after arranging a time and place for us to meet tomorrow morning at the Port, went next to speak with Mical Delmont and Ryle Naceme, and afterward met again with Daniel before heading toward my father's house. Halfway there, I passed the Bameritan Hyatt and saw a man get out of a black government car and walk inside. I recognized the man from his photograph in the papers, rode my bike around back, entered the hotel through the kitchen and used the in-house phone to track his room on the sixth floor. "Please, leave me be," Leo Covings complained of too many disturbances when I knocked. I explained who I was, told him of my connection to the strike and that I had some news he might find of interest. After a few seconds, he let me in.

I arrived at my father's house an hour later. The plan to seize the main warehouse had come together and my father wanted to discuss moving women and children from the capital. Deceiving him was not anything I did well. Twice I found him staring at me and angled my face away in order to be only half-exposed.

Just after 10 p.m. I said goodnight and came outside. I was eager to get back across town to Katima and Daniel and the others, but Don Pendar surprised me, was waiting with my bike already in the back of his car. "Come on, I'll take you home." He left the headlights dark for several blocks before bringing us out of the neighborhood and onto the numbered streets. While he drove, his fingers squeezed and released the wheel. I saw the line of his jaw, the bone and muscle in shadow as we passed under the moon. My first thought was that he'd heard about the rally, and I was prepared to deny any knowledge if he asked. He made no reference however, said only, "When all of this is over, André."

"We'll have a drink."

"It's a date," he looked at me, then back at the road. His voice was pitched as always, his words rushed as if he couldn't get them out fast enough. He started talking about Teddy, about necessity and sacrifice, all the cliched terms those who'd never been to war chattered on about. I let him continue for a minute, was staring at my hands when he said, "It's a good plan." He waited for me to reply, but I decided to let the comment pass. Never easily put off, Don Pendar persisted. "Don't you think?"

"Does it matter what I think?"

"Of course."

"If you're looking for reassurances."

He shook his head. "I know how it seems sometimes between us, André, but I'm always interested in what you have to say."

"Now that I've agreed to help," I used my bluff. "You listen when its convenient, when it's what you want to hear."

"It's a perfect plan," he ignored me, answered as he wanted. I grew annoyed and couldn't keep from saying, "No, it's not. It's a risk at best. That's all it is."

"It doesn't matter," Don Pendar started in again, presented examples from history, revolutions that seemed on their face to support his claim. I started my dissent, but he interrupted and wanted to know, "Can I ask you something else?"

"That depends."

"About the War of the Winds. Were you scared?"

I turned on my seat, rubbed the sweat from the top of my head, nearly laughed but caught myself and answered, "You're asking me this now?"

"It doesn't change anything," he was quick to tell me. "I'm just curious."

"Every one of us was scared," I let him know. "Every day. Emilo and Justin. All of us."

Don Pendar thought about this, then said, "Good." Five minutes later he pulled the car onto my street and parked against the curb. We stayed silent for a time. I started getting out of the car then stopped myself and told him, "The worst fear a man can have is discovering what he believes in with all his heart is wrong."

There followed only the briefest pause before Don Pendar looked at me again. For just a second his features softened, a sense of near concession before he stiffened, a defense drawn so tight the skin on his cheeks and around his mouth grew harder as he said, "And so we fight to make sure that never happens." He wiped his face with both hands. When he glanced at me again his eyes had changed. I said nothing further. He came from the car, removed my bike from the trunk and pushed it toward me. I stood out front after he drove off, the lights on this side of the capital all shut down. After a minute I got on my bike and rode back across town to Daniel's apartment. Our demonstration was set to begin in less than eight hours. Inside, Daniel found candles and we worked with what light we had.

———

Early the next morning, before the first of our neighbors appeared on the street and began walking to the Port, I stood and looked out the bedroom window. The city was quiet still, the sky dark yet clear. Katima came and slipped her arms around me from behind. I relaxed just enough to not let her feel me shake, then went into the bathroom and washed in the bowl of yesterday's water. Downstairs, I lit the stove and boiled tea. We ate the three remaining slices of bread and half an orange before going outside. Our plan was to have everyone approach the Port along a series of side roads, with separate groups coming from different directions, converging on Wenlafte Boulevard and then walking together to the main warehouse. All of our plotting these last three days was a blur. I worried no one would show, that in our haste we'd forgotten something and our effort would come crashing down on our heads. To my great relief, slowly, in small groups, students and neighbors, women in sandals and men in morning sweaters, friends and strangers appeared and began walking with us. Halfway to the Port, our number grew from fifty to a few hundred to over a thousand. Leo Covings sat on the roof of his black car, a cameraman beside him, the sedan gliding carefully around our perimeter, recording our march. The police kept their distance, watched without ordering us to disperse, just as the Chief Inspector promised.

Daniel was waiting when we reached the Port and together we took a quick survey of the area. The space in front of the main warehouse was flat and open, covering some 800 square feet. To show our rally was peaceful and that we weren't there to seize or damage government property, we stopped our march at the curb. I spoke with Cris, then started back through the crowd, on my way to see Bo, who'd set up our webcam in the apartment across the street.

Within the hour more people arrived. Soldiers gathered off to the side. The sun was up, our number now at several thousand, I was ecstatic and stood on a wooden box, a portable microphone in hand as I recited Ghandi quotes I knew by heart: "Pure motives can never justify impure or violent action," and "I believe that it is possible to introduce uncompromising truth and honesty in the political life of (any) country." I recalled what Huxley wrote: "The law of the survival of the fittest is the law for the evolution of the brute, but the law of self-sacrifice is the law of evolution for the man." The people in front of me cheered and encouraged me to go on. I laughed and raised my hands above my head, applauding in turn, confident and well pleased, though no sooner did I repeat the line from Huxley than something odd caught my eye.

There on the south side of Wenlafte Boulevard, three men moved through the crowd. Each had short hair, their stride deliberate, their casual clothes identical to the rest of us except, instead of sandals or ordinary footwear, they had on thick black boots. I watched the tallest of the three men glance up at the window where Bo was filming, saw him look back and signal the others who reached then inside their shirts.

The pop-pop-pop came a half second later. The men aimed their pistols over our heads, the first shots creating chaos. I heard more shots and then the screams. People ran while I waved my arms and shouted for Bo to stop transmitting. The soldiers waiting on the sidelines took their cue from the men dressed to look like us and unloaded into the crowd. Our webcam and Leo Covings' camera recorded everything, exactly as Teddy planned, the headlines around the world tomorrow made to read: "Government Acts To Quash Bloody Coup."

Pushed back, I tried to find Katima and Ali. More soldiers appeared out of nowhere while everyone looked to escape. I came through a clearing in the crowd, hurried toward the front, shouted for Katima, turned and spotted Don Pendar standing there. "Run!" I yelled. "Go! Go!" but he paid no attention, was watching me, not angrily or in any sort of way I would have expected. I saw him roll his hands over, gently at first, his eyes going wide before turning his hands back around and balling his fingers into fists. I shouted again but he was already charging toward a group of soldiers, nearly reaching them only to have his body jerk and his arms fly out.

The Port was filled by then with jeeps and trucks giving chase, cutting off exit routes, circling the main warehouse with sirens and horns blaring. Don Pendar went down to his knees, his arms limp, the front of his shirt alive and wet. I dropped with him, held his head in my lap as a jeep flew past us then doubled back. The soldier in charge climbed out, called me by name, ordered me to, "Get up, Mafante!"

I remained as before, ran my hand through Don Pendar's hair, slowly and gently so. The hard warm stone of the road beneath us cut my knees. At that distance I couldn't see my tower, though I imagined her rising behind me, the photographs of Tamina and old clippings. I pictured my children, Anita and Ali, saw Katima as she lay in bed that

morning. The stain running onto my legs from Don
Pendar's chest was different from the blood as I bit
at the sides of my mouth. My shaved head burned
beneath the sun. In Jallianwalla Bagh, Gandhi's
mistake allowed British soldiers to slaughter hundreds of unarmed Indians who'd gathered peacefully
in the gardens. Three years later, when Gandhi was
arrested in Bardoli on new charges of sedition, he
was kneeling in prayer with a group of Ashramites
as the police came and took him away.

"I would regard the observance of a perfect
peace on my arrest as a mark of high honor paid
to me by my countrymen," Gandhi wrote of his
time at Sabarmati prison. I tried to imagine the
same happening now in Bamerita but already the
men from the capital were rushing the Port. When
I struggled to pray, none of the right words came
out. I called for Katima while the soldiers pulled
me to my feet, bound me hand and foot and tossed
me into the rear of their jeep as penalty for my
nonsense. I refused to curse them out loud, though
in my heart everything was clear and for this, too,
I was struck hard and briefly made to sleep.

BOOK 2

CHAPTER 9

Anita Mafante reached the Madeira Islands a week after her father's arrest. She sat at a table overlooking the ocean. In front of her was a sea bass cooked in a syrupy lemon sauce, the head and teeth still intact so that, laid out in the center of the serving plate, the fish stared up with an air of fierce surprise. Anita peeled the skin nearest the belly, cut through and ate the meat below.

Nick Wyle sat facing the sun. The food on his plate was rice and corn and bits of tuna. Nick's father, Charles, leaned in to pour more wine. A career consul to the region, assigned to minor ports, Charles had lived in Madeira twelve years. A plenipotentiary in an outpost requiring little by way of serious investment, he adopted to the lulls, followed developments in Bamerita from a distance, the war outside his jurisdiction yet close enough still for him to say, "The shit has hit." He describe the fighting after the ambush at the Port, how the NBDF was a day's march outside the capital when the shooting began. "Men with pistols."

"Soldiers."

"This isn't how it looked on film."

"But we know who it was."

"What do we know?" Charles described other men with hunting rifles racing from their homes, while the rebels from the hills established strongholds, were overrun and fell back, reassembled and shifted positions again and again. "Your father," Charles continued, apologized for having no further news. "The government has closed off all travel. Your grandfather is under house arrest, your brother missing. The kettle has blown. These are not conditions one should return to." He wore a slightly rumpled suit, his brown hair combed back, the collar of his shirt unstarched, his jacket with an ancient shine. He glanced at his son, took another sip of wine before refocusing on Anita. "I'd advise you not to go." Having already agreed to help, he felt he'd earned the right to offer his opinion. "What is it you hope to accomplish? What exactly are your plans?" His tone was firm. He raised his eyebrows in a way that let Anita know he held her accountable for involving Nick.

Anita rolled her wrists so that her knife and fork stood straight. She tipped her head just enough so that the breeze from the sea caught her hair and moved it in waves beneath the moon. She had her mother's features, Tamina's eyes and chin given the slightest cleft, her cheeks cut in toward the corners of her mouth which was pink and softly shaded. Nick's face was fuller, more round with light brown hair, his nose thick at the ridge yet otherwise fine, his eyes deep and green. His skin was not as dark as Anita's, though he spent much of his days outdoors. Peripatetic, raised in several ports of call and cities far removed from the States, he took up his mother's career as a photo journalist, spent weeks in Nigeria, was in the Kashmiri Valley as the pilgrims hiked to Amarnath Cave and the shrine of Lord Shiva, had - by 28 - added film to his resume, hired by CAN - Cable America Network - to cover developments in Afghanistan, Iraq, Liberia, Somalia, Madrid and Iran.

Anita tapped the table and said in answer to Charles, "I'm going home." Nick reached and gently touched her wrist, watched her set the knife down. Charles Wyle gave a nod and pushed his own fish aside. "You'll need connections in order to make appeals for your family." He mentioned this to let them know his cooperation was still there if they were determined to go. "I can put you in touch with Erik Dukette, the American Consul."

Anita thanked him but said, "It's probably not a good idea for anyone to know we're there just yet."

"Friends only," Nick agreed.

"Don't worry," Charles waved them both off, reminded Nick how far back he and Dukette went, assured them, "On my word, Erik can be trusted."

———

If viewed from the road below, Moulane Prison has the look of an old castle, the structure large and primal, built years ago by Sir Albert Moulane just after Bamerita's sixth revolution, the War of the Barrows. Sir Albert made his fortune in shipping, his fleet of schooners used to transport slaves, tusks of poached ivory and snuff. The main house is solid stone and rises mammoth above the hillside overlooking the water, three miles east of the capital. Following the War of the Barrows, in 1895, the property was converted into a retreat for the new prime minister who - along with his mistress and two children - was beheaded six years later in yet another coup. For many years the grounds fell into disrepair until, under Teddy, Moulane was recast as a penitentiary, the rooms turned into cages, the wine cellar a dungeon where I'm kept now.

I sit in the dark, the cool clay of the earth beneath me. The walls are hard silt reinforced by mortar, what light there is comes through the small window cut high on the wall outside my cell, some twelve feet away. I try and gauge the hour by the sun which filters in briefly but brings mostly shadow. At night the darkness is so complete I lay in the center of my cell where, even with my eyes wide, I see absolutely nothing.

My guards are told who I am and how to treat me. I'm routinely pushed about, struck and spit on. The food they bring is mixed with dirt and chiggers. One game they like to play involves storming downstairs late at night with lanterns lit, carrying boards and sticks. They hand me a stick and place wagers on the time it takes me to kill a rat. "Come on, come on!" I'm told to use my blanket to trap the rats which are large and swift and difficult to corner. The soldiers say I'll be given extra food if I'm successful and treated severely if I fail. Money is bet and rules set up. I'm allowed four tosses with my blanket before I've lost. The light complicates matters as the rats scatter while I hunt them down. The guards scream at me to, "Go! Go!" and block the rats' escape with boards along the bottom of my cell. Even when I do my best, it's impossible for me to win. No matter how well I execute the challenge, there's always a guard who's lost his bet and quick to take his anger out

on me. The winners, in turn, offer no protection.
Not once have I received extra food, and no matter
what, I wind up punished for my effort.

Days pass. I think of Don Pendar and what
he could have said to me at the Port, how "Here's
the thing you feared most, André, the faith in your
heart proved wrong." My capture is deserved, the
guilt I feel worse than any physical torture, and
still I'm no martyr and wish simply for all of this
to be done. The hairs on my once shaved head are
growing out like spikes, I tug in an effort to make
them longer. Ashamed, I imagine what I look like
and who could recognize me now.

The guards stomp their feet above me, their
booted strides landing heavy enough to cause bits
of mud and dust to fall from my ceiling. In the
dark, I listen when they talk. Sometimes I hear
what sounds like women weeping, the sobs passing
through the walls as if channelled from a great
distance. I wonder if there are actually any female
prisoners in the cages upstairs, or if the guards
have brought in women for their own amusement.
From where I am, I picture all the worst.

At some point each night the guards bring
another prisoner downstairs. These men are not
NBDF supporters but criminals arrested and
ordered to beat me. They do as they're told, hit
me with their fists, use their elbows and fingers
to jab and gouge and kick me when their arms get
tired. The last man here has pounded my head
and chest, opened old wounds, bruised my spine
and twisted my arms until ligament and bone are
wrenched. The guards have told him to keep me
awake, but he can't resist the dark, shoves me into
a corner, shouts at me, "Don't move," and lays
down to rest. I wait until I'm sure he's asleep, and

once the aches in my body settle into a single puls-
ing sting, I try to doze as well. I wake a few hours
later to the sound of the guards turning the key
again at the top of the stairs. The man jumps up at
the last moment and slaps me once in the ear. The
guards shine their lantern in on us, laugh as I stumble
against the bars, and jabbing at me with their rifles,
say "Enough, enough. So early in the morning."

Alone again, I sit with my legs extended and
arms laid flat in my lap. My bare feet are covered
with the blanket as protection from the rats. I try
and stand but find I can barely shift my shoulders
away from the bars, my aches and sores too much.
I think again how Gandhi joked of his first time in
prison, "It will give me a quiet and physical rest
which perhaps I deserve," and how I feel nothing like
this, am convinced of just the opposite. I picture
Katima, compare my decisions to those of Alina Pienkowska in Gdansk and how was it the soldiers in
Poland didn't fire on the shipyard while here at the
Port everything went so wrong? What did I miss or
refuse to consider? The questions in the dark are
the same each day. I sit back against the wall and
wait for answers.

———

The day before the rally, Ali took the money
his father gave him and sent word to Evan Moore.
Final preparations were made, supplies gathered
and routes checked. That night, Ali and Feona sat
near the ridge at the end of the playground, overlooking the northern half of the city. The moon
above was split through its center like a frosted
slice of white cake. "I should go with you," Feona
had her fingers spread in the dry green grass.

Ali discouraged her, said "The others will need you here." He ran his left hand up and down Feona's leg. Sleeping at All Kings, they'd not made love for some time. Moments outside acquired gravity, intimacy found in small details. Like Katima, Feona had cut her hair short, straight and well above her shoulders. Ali liked the way her features stood out now, her face perfectly exposed, an elegant fish swimming closer to the surface of the water.

Early the next morning Ali headed toward Wenlafte Boulevard as he promised his father. A huge crowd had already gathered near the main warehouse. Ali passed through the center, searching and spotting familiar faces, until he was caught suddenly in the rush and fire as the first shots rang out. Knocked down by people trying to flee, unable to find his father as more soldiers jumped out from where they were hiding, Ali's concerns shifted to All Kings. He dashed back, arriving behind three of the older boys who were already there describing the attack.

Several children cried, their hands in flight about their faces, while the younger ones were simply confused, ran around the playground, knowing something dangerous and exciting had happened but unsure what. Feona was trying to pull everyone together as Ali raced up, sweating and panting, bending forward with hands on knees. Everyone stopped and waited for him to say something. He stood slowly, trying not to tremble as he told them, "Ok. Alright. Here's what we're going to do."

Convinced the army would raid the school as the fighting spread, the soldiers looking to use the grounds as a strategic hold, Ali sent five boys to watch the roads. He had Feona organize the children, packing clothes and loading foods into bags and boxes not too heavy to carry. "Keep everyone here," he went inside and filled a 3-gallon container with gas from their reserve. The old school bus used before the strike was parked behind a locked fence at Demucho's Garage a half mile west of All Kings. Ali ran as best he could with the container of gas clutched to his chest. After climbing the fence, he pitched a rock through the window of the office and took the keys.

Scavengers had syphoned the bus tank dry. Even with the gas Ali brought the engine took a minute to turn. He shifted and drove through the locked gate back onto the road. Feona had everyone outside again, 120 kids, four times the number originally planned to pass through Kaprischo Point. Ali pulled up, spoke with the oldest boys, told them where to go and who to contact. The remaining children were hurried onto the bus as Ali changed quickly into a dry t-shirt, boots and socks. Supplies were loaded in the aisle, the last two containers of gas dragged out and emptied into the tank.

The quickest way to Kaprischo Point was south through the center of the capital. All the central routes were sure to be closed by now however, sending Ali north, then east, circling along the outer edge of the city until he reached the highway. The sounds of the fighting were less ominous the further they drove. Ali looked in the rearview mirror, found Feona sitting with the children playing some sort of word game. Such innocence seemed surreal, and for a moment he pretended they were on holiday, taking a leisurely drive to the country. Few cars were on the road and this, too, seemed a good omen.

Perhaps it was the size of the bus and possibility of what they might be carrying, but when three military trucks appeared on the opposite side of the road, the driver of the lead truck cut across the median and force Ali to brake. Six soldiers jumped out, beat their rifles against the sides and ordered everyone out.

Ali tried to pocket the keys but the first soldier pushed his way through the door and grabbed them. Feona and the children were herded together to the shoulder of the road, the bus then driven across the highway. The sergeant in charge had a pear-shaped head, his cheeks pockmarked and eyes deeply darkened. Ali presented his wallet, said "We're from All Kings. I was told to drive the children out to Terbulune, to work on the General's farms. Is there a problem?" For his effort he received a blow hard across the flat of his back.

His ID was kicked through the dirt. The children wailed and were shouted at in turn by the sergeant. The woods ran parallel to the road, up a wide incline, some eighty yards from the highway, separated by a stretch of grass and weeds. At the top of the rise trees extended back. The sergeant ordered the children and Feona to move in a line facing him. Ali was lifted and shoved in the center. Feona held three of the smallest boys behind her as the soldiers came and raised their rifles.

When the first volley of shots hit and echoed in the road, two of the soldiers dropped while the others dove down. Ali spun back and began pushing the children sideways, screaming for them to, "Run!" More shots from the woods landed in the dirt before the soldiers rolled and returned fire. The trucks on the opposite side of the highway raced across the divide, the children in the tall grass sprinting for the trees as the men gave cover.

Ali found Feona and ran with her through the weeds, his hands on her hips all but lifting her from behind. He did not let go even as his side flashed hot, the jolt causing him to stumble for several strides. Feona felt the shift in his grip and called out, her voice giving him something to float upon as he struggled to regain his balance, resetting his hands while telling her not to stop.

Deep over rock and weed, shrub and brush and dirt gone dry in the heat, the children scattered from the soldiers' fire. As they reached the woods, the wound in Ali's side was a fist hole breach. Feona helped lay him down. How strange he felt, so pleased and sad and tired. He stared at her features, terrified and lovely. His heart pounded, his fingers and feet passing from warm to cool. Laid out on bristle torn from the brush, the sky through the branches a silver-blue, he stared, nearly smiling, curious and wistful, surprised he never noticed before how much Feona looked like Tamina.

CHAPTER 10

From Madeira, travelling with false papers and the passports Charles Wyle provided, Anita and Nick entered the Port by way of a ship delivering canned goods and flour. They waited until dark then left the deck and walked down Wenlafte Boulevard, past buildings boarded and damaged by gunfire. A smell in the air not of the sea but sulphur and waste. Teddy had lifted the curfew, creating a false sense of normalcy as more shops and restaurants opened and public transportation was provided on the hour. Soldiers manned checkpoints and marched on patrol. Anita and Nick were asked for ID, made to unzip their duffle, the soldiers taking the cigarettes Nick left on top before letting them pass. They caught the first bus west toward the University, Anita sitting by the window, Nick holding her hand.

Last summer, standing in line for tickets to see Alice Coltrane, they struck up a conversation. Three months later Anita moved into Nick's apartment on the west side, a short subway ride from Columbia and her graduate studies. The celerity of their affair seemed at times ripe for flaring out, like one of those silver sparklers lit and briefly glowing. Such velocity also provided its own adhesion, a sort of emotional centrifugal force. Anita did not speak at first of love, her focus on finishing school and returning home. Nick knew better than to force the issue, the effort like trying to pull puffs of smoke from the air and stuff them in one's pocket.

He left for five days on assignment, sent to film the evacuation of 11,000 residents living near Mount Merapi in Yogyakarta, Indonesia as the mountain neared eruption. Anita remembered the shifts in the ground from her childhood, as Bamerita beneath her seemed to roll at times like a great fish. Two hours before Nick's flight was due to land back in New York, she went and sat at the airport, surprised by her need and how eager she was to tell him. That spring they discussed Nick's moving to Bamerita. He suggested to CAN that he work for them full-time based overseas, a possibility taken under advisement.

The bus left them near Seventh Street, in front of the student apartments where Anita lived her final year as an undergraduate. The buildings were dark, all the students having scattered after the rally. Anita stood with Nick, counted up to the window of her old apartment. The lobby was black and filled with dank, fusty air, the apartment empty and unlocked. Nick found a flashlight in their duffle while Anita opened the window and leaned outside. "It isn't what I expected," she said. The gunfire heard earlier in the distance had stopped, the silence itself unsettling.

The first time Nick was sent to film a war he'd felt the same, having anticipated infinite carnage, riots and explosions and finding then how much of war was waiting. Anita could see the black shapes of buildings on campus, the angle from the window cutting off her view of the old neighborhood to the north. "Here," she moved from the window, lifted her shirt so Nick could peel the tape on her back. He kissed the spot where they'd hidden their money before leaving the ship, the tape turning Anita's flesh pink. She shifted behind him, knelt on the bed, raised his shirt and stripped off a similar pack. After this, she slid beneath his arms and into his lap. Reaching, she touched the side of his cheek. He kissed her fingers as they came near his mouth. She thought of her father, her brother and grandfather, said of her friends, of Tobias Pemu whom they managed to contact from Madeira, "We should call now. He's probably waiting."

"We just got here," Nick held her hips. "They're supposed to find us. That was the plan. We don't know what their situation is. Let's get our bearings first."

"What bearings?" Anita leaned back. "We're here."

"I'm only saying," Nick watched her stand, catching and losing her in the glow of the flashlight. "If you want to help your dad," he gave her this to think about, said "We need to be careful. We have to consider the things we do now. Making phone calls when we don't know the lay of the land is dangerous."

"The only way we can know what's going on is to get in touch with people," Anita went back to the window.

Nick mentioned his father's suggestion. "There's always Dukette. Maybe the American Consul's not such a bad place to start." He turned on the tap in the bathroom, hoping for water but getting nothing more than a hollow echo from the pipes. Anita on the floor, fished through their duffle in search of the cell phone Charles had given them. Nick's camera was also hidden inside, a Canon ZR50 MC with SD memory cards the soldiers missed when stealing the cigarettes. Nick came back into the bedroom, saw Anita remove the phone and start to dial. "I thought we were going to wait."

"I'll just let it ring once, to let them know we're here." Her face was lit in profile as she sat beside the duffle. "Will it work with the electricity off?" she asked about the phone.

Nick saw the way her shoulders rolled, beautiful and smooth, her arms and legs loose, their stretch and curl tempting him to forget everything and see if she'd make love to him there on the floor. He touched her neck, tugged gently at her hair, was about to tell her how the phones ran on a different electrical line than the lights when he heard sounds from the stairs, and then in the hallway, footsteps closer still outside the door. He grabbed the flashlight, thinking soldiers had spotted the glow from outside, while Anita dropped the phone back in the duffle and hurried to the front room. Expecting Tobias, she found Kart instead, standing with hands out. "Anita Mafante. A.M. radio," he called her as he used to, said "Aren't you a sight for everything sore."

———

The window on the far wall outside my cell is never opened. The soldiers as they come downstairs curse the smell, yell "Shit!" then laugh at this before holding their breath and making me remove my own bucket. The only chance I have for fresh air is on days I'm brought into the yard and ordered to run. The grounds are unkept, with thorns and thistle. The hillside in the distance is beautiful. My bare feet are bruised and brittle and bleed over the stones. As best I can, I concentrate on the warm sun against my skin, the smell of the water just beyond the walls, and the clean air I pull into my lungs.

I'm shouted at to run faster and faster until my body shakes and I fall to my knees. Each time I do this, I'm yanked up, told to keep running, only to stumble again. The guards swear and slap me hard with their rifles, kick me with their boots and drag me to my feet. After, I'm told to strip and allowed to wash with dirty water poured inside a wooden bowl. On days I'm brought outside, I also try to defecate so as not to keep filling my cell with waste, though mostly this, too, is refused me.

When my time is over, I'm marched back down the stairs, shoved from behind and returned underground. For several seconds in the dark the sensation of the sunlight in the yard lingers. I try holding on for as long as I can but she fades regardless. My ribs ache as I sink and sit on the floor. The pain in my right hip is sharp and shoots violent charges down my leg and through my feet. My toenails are thick and black and curl inward like nervous animals looking for a place to burrow. I calm my breathing with thoughts of Katima, imagine her safe and unharmed, remind myself that she's resilient, resourceful and clever, and still I worry, know from experience all that can happen.

By late afternoon I receive my only food of the day, a brownish stew with lumps of cornmeal, meat fat, a few cubes of vegetable and insects which have invaded the mix. Despite the contents, I eat hungrily. A new prisoner is brought down soon after I finish eating. This man is small, all elbows and knees. He pounces like a snake off its coil, hits my chest, pulls and twists my arms, grabs my ears and scratches my cheek. "Brarr!" he shoves me back, curses because I've no shoes for him to steal, snatches up my empty food bowl and flings it at my head. I duck, turn and stare at his face. Although his cheeks are covered with flecks of black whiskers, and his mouth is filled with worn brown teeth, he appears boyish, if not youthful then troll-like. His eyes are dark, his skin yellow-grey. I raise my hands in defense as he moves toward me again. "Wait, please." I ask, "What have they told you? Do you know who I am?"

The man slaps me hard before asking, "Why should I care?"

I tell him my name nonetheless and the man looks at me in disbelief. "The tower guy?"

"That's right."

He spits. "Mafante's dead," he says. "They tore his tower down," and finding the softness beneath my ribs, he punches me again, tells me to, "Shut the fuck up!"

I accuse him of being the guards' stooge and he hits me harder still, stopping only when he tires and orders me to, "Stay here!" He shoves me against the bars, looks at me strangely for a moment, appears on the verge of saying something, only to curse again and slip off to sleep. I watch him then, want to forgive the troll-man. Gandhi says mercy is the key to Satyagrahi, but somehow my extending pardon seems misplaced. Who am I to absolve anyone? When the guards return later the man is still sleeping. I hear them coming but don't call out. The guards drag the troll-man off and he shrieks in horror. I listen above me to the sounds behind the heavy door locking, immediately regret what I've done and ask forgiveness but there's no one here.

More time passes. The minor light through my window fades until all is dark with just a hint of stars shining in the distance. I doze until something wakes me. Whistles are blown, alarms ring in the cells above my head, a stampede of boots and soldiers shouting. The door at the top of the stairs is thrown open and more than a dozen prisoners are brought down. An equal number of guards follows close behind. The space outside my cell is crammed, the prisoners shoved against the north wall, the guards punching and shouting at them to, "Shut up! Shut up!"

The sound of pop and fire comes from the yard. Half the men fall silent while the others shake and weep. A tense confusion lasts until a new alarm goes off and the prisoners are ordered back upstairs. They exhale collectively with great relief. The guards laugh, as if everything has been a game they've played together. I remain pressed against the front of my cage, stare up at the small window where starlight shows a series of feet moving by. The men huddled in front of me not three minutes before realize now and dance in the yard as a new crack and echo takes them down.

Everything goes quiet after this. Even the guards are silent. The prisoners have fallen so that I can see only the soles of their feet. I stand with my face pressed against the bars. A minute later I sink and reach for my blanket, stay this way until morning. More time passes. I imagine the prison empty, the soldiers told to leave me behind, my final days spent alone in the dark, starving until the rats finish me off. The idea creates something outside of panic. My hunger is sour, I breathe hard, fill my belly with air. I think again of the men last night, remember Brahmacharya and an essay by Ghandi which began, "During these days I walked up and down the streets of Calcutta," and included a description of sacrificial sheep's blood flowing in a stream after their offering at a temple in Kali. I want to convince myself the men are this, all innocent sheep, but know their innocence is irrelevant. Suddenly the door at the top of the stairs opens and two guards come down.

Instead of being brought into the yard and forced to run, my hands are cuffed this time, my ankles shackled as I'm lead inside the main floor of the prison. The space is vast with dozens of cages set around the perimeter of what was once the ballroom and dining area of the Moulane Estate. I've never seen this part of the prison. Wooden planks are placed across the top of the lower cells and a second row added over them. A narrow scaffolding built in the interior creates a catwalk on which the guards patrol. The light upstairs causes me to squint. I'm pushed from behind, told to keep moving, the weight of the chains slowing my walk. I see men from the demonstration, students and others, crowded three and four inside each cage. The smell is of sweat and waste, the floors damp, the air nearly as stale as below.

The Captain of the Guards stands at the front of the main hall. Thin and tall, with pale cheeks and dark hair beneath his military cap, his uniform is clean and well tailored, yet sags on him slightly like a loose second skin. He holds a faded blue cloth up in front of his face and stares at me over the top of his hand. I look away, focus on the cages.

I suspect, after last night, the Captain plans to parade me about as proof to the others that any further fighting is futile, the revolt inside the prison having failed, our revolution outside lost, my capture evidence of this. I regret being used for such a purpose, hope my whiskered face, torn and soiled clothes, hunched shoulders and wild hair make me unrecognizable. The men stare through their bars just the same, curious and eager to get a better look, first one and then another saying, "Mafante? André Mafante?" until everyone is stirring and the guards leave me to walk on my own.

I slump my shoulders that much more, become smaller, shake my head and wish to hide. Those who know me continue to chant, encourage the others. The cages allow them to see me from all sides. Their voices roll together, merge from sporadic bursts into a united and rhythmic cadence. "Ma-fant-e!" Hands begin to clap and beat against the bars as more men join in. "Ma-fant-e! Ma-fant-e!" The Captain stiffens and readies his guards.

The men do not cheer for me, of course, but for who they think I am. My reputation unifies us. Those who supported our strike and the rally, and others who care for nothing but revolution and are convinced the demonstration was intended to kick start the war, all together cheer, "Ma-fant-e!" If I'm blamed for the disaster at the Port no one says a word. The reaction is much different than what the Captain expected, the spirit of the caged men causing me to forget myself briefly and I raise my chained arms, moved by their sentiment. Instead of quieting them, I encourage them to change their chant to, "NBDF! NBDF!" Immediately the prisoners echo my shouts. The Captain signals and the guards rush in and drag me off.

———

Katima near the coves, collects driftwood and seaweed strong enough to use as twine. The foundation of the tower she is making is buried deep and away from the tide, close to the rocks where she can climb above the sand and attach one piece of wood to another. She shifts from dune to rock to standing atop the coves, climbing higher on the lip of the cliff and building upward.

Once the rally collapsed into riot, as the soldiers drove André off and Katima saw only his legs in the rear of the jeep, she ran from the Port up and down the streets, trying to follow. By evening she'd attempted to reach Davi, Josh Durret, Dr. Bernarr and Ali, had gone to the Plaza where raw footage from the morning appeared on Teddy's movie screen, spliced together with new scenes shot in documentary fashion; a thriller culled with flashpoints and characters Leo Covings created to give backdrop to the latest rebellion, the War of the Cameras.

The idea for the film came to Leo after André Mafante showed up and asked for help recording the rally. Cinema verite. Flesh on the screen. There was something to be said for the integrity of the extemporaneous. Of course, to make a great movie Leo knew the action must be directed. Even the brilliant Albert Maysles turned and twisted subject and setting to get exactly what he wanted in his seminal film 'Salesman.' To mix fact and fiction, real time and staged, required a certain degree of scripting. Truth couldn't be allowed to unfold on its own without everything getting messy. "What if?" Leo called the States before passing his ideas on to Teddy who danced a spirited two-step and thought the idea genius.

Each morning Katima went to stand outside Moulane Prison where other women in black dress arrived on buses, in cars and by foot. They held up pictures of their missing sons, brothers and husbands, their heads covered by scarves and veils as if already grieving the dead. Katima refused to wear the same, showed up instead in what she knew André liked: t-shirts and shorts, cotton skirts and soft blue jeans. By 9:00 a.m. she'd leave Moulane in André's car and go to the train station near Verone. Teddy assigned soldiers to monitor her movements, while Katima in turn spent much of her days in a series of misdirection.

From Verone she took the train inland to Duratchi, a small trading post founded years ago by local farmers. The corporal assigned to follow her from the train kept six paces behind as she went to a nearby restaurant and had tea. Afterward she bought stamps and mailed two letters at the post office. The letters were sent to unoccupied addresses, messages for presumed NBDF supporters meant to be intercepted by Teddy. Each missive contained erroneous reference to plans and movements by the rebels. Two and three times a week she posted the letters, lead soldiers through the capital, stopped outside the city at deserted farms and back again at empty houses the government would later raid and find nothing.

The same corporal follows Katima from Duratchi, drives behind as she heads east to the coast where the scent of salt water fills the air and the sight of gulls can be seen dipping and gliding in the horizon. The corporal sits in the open sand, some thirty yards away from where Katima is working. He waits and watches. From the cliff Katima's climbed, braced out over the edge, she attaches another piece of driftwood, using seaweed and twine she has brought from the car. Her tower is a precarious makeshift construct, more of a rod pointing skyward from the sands, wavering in the wind and unlikely to withstand the winter. Still she continues, the exercise a therapy. When the soldiers first arrived at the house, not ten hours after the attack at the Port, wielding saws and chains and hand axes to tear André's tower down, Katima stood in the yard howling. Held back by friends, she expected to be arrested but the soldiers ignored her, left her standing among the ruins as the tower crashed and was cut into smaller pieces, hacked again and again until little more than memory remained.

A breeze from the sea catches the latest clipping Katima is trying to attach, a piece on Chakufwa Chihana, Malawi's leading pro-democracy campaigner whose underground political movement ousted Malawi's long standing dictator, Kamuza Banda, in 1994. Katima has the top of the steeple bowed, grabs for the paper as it floats from her hand, finds herself lifted and drawn forward, dangling for a moment above the cliff, raised as light and effortless as if she doesn't exist at all. The strength of the rod surprises her, that it can carry her this way, up and out from the cliff and toward the water.

The corporal on the sand stands and moves toward the rocks. The paper blowing down glides and lands at his feet. Katima kicks her legs, hangs then lands back on the cliff. In the moment before, sailing above, André's voice kept her from releasing prematurely. She stares down, the shaft straight again, the corporal beneath her clutching the paper, raising it up and showing it to her as if he has found something valuable they both have been searching for. He walks toward the base of the tower, reads then places the clipping in among the others, tucks it behind an older piece, turns and walks back to where he was sitting. Katima on top of the cove, retraces her steps across the cliff, lifts her head and examines the wood, looks toward the soldier and once more at the tower, wondering in a way she hasn't until that very second how high must she build and how far will it go?

———

———

The house Kart brought Anita and Nick to was owned by Verne Odete. Odete was a chemist, researching uses for hypnotics in surgical procedures, diethylmalonyl urea - or diethylbarbituric acid $(C2H5)2C-Co\ NH/1CO$ - mixed with sodium ethylate, ethyl iodide, or the silver salt of malonyl urea. Under Teddy, all Verne's research was shut down, the new government interested only in drugs which brought immediate profit. ("Give us Viagra! Phenodal! Vicadin! Prozac!") The day Emilo had his feet crushed in the Plaza, Verne offered his house as a safe haven for the NBDF. Kart came to Verne after the soldiers arrested Kara and Angeline, kicked two holes in the drywall off the kitchen, drank half a bottle of cheap mescal and was only prevented from heading back out by the veronal Verne put in his glass.

On the porch was a blue rubber welcome mat. Tobias unloaded a box of canned goods from the trunk of the car, spoke with Kart then disappeared back outside. In each of the three bedrooms, mattresses were laid out among boxes, books and clothes. Nick carried their duffle upstairs, while Anita remained in the front room. Kart sat on the grey couch, hunched over the low table where a map and several large diagrams were spread out. "This is where we are," he said, and pointing to three more streets where the NBDF had safe houses, waved his hand and told her, "The rest is open water."

Anita asked about her father, about Ali and her grandfather, the information Kart provided not so much more than what Charles Wyle had gathered in Madeira. "Not to worry," he tapped the pile of diagrams. "We have plans." When Anita wondered what specifically, Kart flipped to the diagrams' middle pages which contained detailed schematics for several of the ministries. "These are the end game," he gave her a moment to understand, then turned the diagrams over and said, "Come on."

In the basement Avene Delu and Maria Masombi sat working at a long metal table. The chairs were wood, the light overhead bright. A heater in the corner was used to keep the room dry. Kart introduced Anita to the others. Spread across the table were supplies of gunpowder, fuses and wires, metal and cardboard cylinders, potassium nitrate, charcoal and sulfur, nitro cellulose in a separate box. Avene worked with the wires of what once appeared to be the inside of a clock, attaching tiny transmitters and a square battery to create a timed charge.

Kart picked up a freshly finished stick of dynamite and pointed for Anita to sit in the chair beside Maria. "If you're looking to help," he had Maria show her what to do. Nick came down and stood at the bottom of the stairs. Kart took a toothpick from his pocket, turned it with his tongue, brought it completely inside his mouth and out again. "What about you, boyfriend?" he gestured toward the table. "You ready to get your hands dirty?"

Nick listened to the others talk. ("What are your plans?" his father had asked.) He heard Maria laugh as she told of Avene's teaching her how to build a timer. "I kept setting off the alarm and everyone was sure I'd blow up the house." All their chatter was informal. They seemed quite clearly to be enjoying themselves. Nick felt his shoulders knot. He looked at Anita again, waited until she glanced up at him, smiled and resumed working. He remained standing back at the stairs. Kart saw and slid closer to Anita's chair.

CHAPTER 11

D avi Suntu sat in buddha pose, on cool grass and briar, his legs folded with knees arched to the sides. His belly perfectly centered, his shirt torn in front, exposed soft brown flesh. An hour before the rally, the soldiers came and removed him from bed. If not for his wrists tied tight and secured behind his back, his position would have seemed serene. The soldiers stood together, some fifteen feet away, a man and boy in faded green uniforms and black boots damp with dew. Each finished a cigarette, their rifles resting against their legs. The old soldier told a joke about a woman and a three-legged German shepherd. The boy kicked at the dirt, embarrassed. Davi looked past them, toward trees in the distance and birds darting curious through branches deep in the woods.

A third man with a camera stationed himself off to the side, unobtrusive. The older soldier crushed out his cigarette, said something to the younger one. Davi kept his focus elsewhere, on the sun and shadows, how the breeze through the branches made both light and dark dance across the ground. His legs beneath him were nearly numb, he shifted his hips, wobbling with his hands behind him like a wooden toy. On a nearby branch, a white winged moth or perhaps a butterfly landed on a solitary orange leaf. Davi stared. The way of a buddha is to stay present and be love. The younger soldier moved forward. Davi saw this and did his best to smile. There was in the boy's face such youth and promise. The four noble truths of Buddhism were that life meant suffering; the origin of suffering was attachment; the cessation of suffering was attainable; and the path to the cessation of suffering required sacrifice and personal change. The young soldier measured his distance. Davi offered encouragement, said his first words in more than an hour. "Perhaps closer will make things easier." He looked at the boy, then over at the white moth inside the orange leaf, shuddering and disappearing in a pearl and ivory flash.

———

The rats are disturbed by the rustling of my chains as the guards toss me back in my cell. I fall with my legs bent and head bowed. The men upstairs are no longer chanting and I can only imagine what the guards have done this time to stop them. I crawl on my knees, roll over and lean back against the wall. What a mess I've made again, provoking the others without ever thinking. What was the point? What did I expect to happen? Why couldn't I ignore their early chants and just stand in the center of the floor and be still? What was wrong with showing defiance and non-cooperation by actually resisting and not causing trouble for everyone else for a change? I wonder about this, am trying to decide when the door overhead opens and a yellow-white light shines down.

The air fills with a smell of soap and after-shave. My lungs are confused, and coughing, I shield my head as my cage is unlocked and the light in the Captain's hand covers me. He sets the lantern outside and enters my cell. His keys are on a large ring he tosses near the stairs. I say nothing, continue to watch as he removes the pistol from his holster and surveys the space inside my cage. With his left hand he holds the pale blue cloth in front of his mouth even as he talks. "Please," he points his pistol, gives his narrow shoulders a lift, surprises me by tapping the chain between my wrists. "Go on," he waves toward the open door of my cell and out toward the keys.

I hesitate then drag the chains and step outside, move past the lantern and to the stairs. The Captain remains behind. I sit and unlock the irons around my legs, consider the possibility of my leaping up and slamming the cell door shut, locking the Captain inside. And then? If he doesn't shoot me and I make it upstairs, how will I escape? The Captain seems to know what I'm thinking, gives me a few seconds more then says, "You see, you are capable of restraint."

He comes from my cell, tucks the blue cloth into his pocket, takes the keys and undoes my wrists. "What am I to do with you?" He steps back, kicks the chains away, gives a weary sigh as if the issue is a torture for him. "You weren't supposed to get the others all worked up. I was expecting you to know better. Now I have to start again." He motions me to stand. His teeth are yellow, his breath sour as if some vile illness resides in his gums. I want to say there's nothing to start, that everything is over, but it's clear this isn't what the Captain believes. He puts me back in my cell, closes the door, lifts the lantern and climbs the stairs. "What now?" he repeats, shakes the light and gives another sigh, only to stop halfway up and answer his own question with, "Not to worry. I'll think of something, I'm sure."

I sit for hours after the Captain leaves and try to imagine. The threat is beyond me, is nothing I can guess, and still I can't stop thinking. The darkness inside my cell is venal. In Yeravda Jail, Gandhi wrote how he used his imprisonment for worship, referred to his cell as his 'mandir,' his temple in which he concentrated on forms of self-improvement and training himself to feel happy. Such horse shit, I'm convinced now. Gandhi in prison took lime juice and honey after 4:00 a.m. prayers, wrote and read and what sort of confinement is that? "We must make the best possible use of the invaluable leisure in jail," he wrote and wouldn't that be easy if I was somewhere other than under-ground in a dirt walled cellar with a bucket full of piss?

I'm again upset with myself for feeling this way and am in the process of trying to regain my strength when the silence above at long last gives way and I hear familiar noises, thumps and echoes, heavy objects dragged and men with hoarse, impatient voices barking. This time as the door at the top of the stairs opens, the light shined down is brighter than the Captain's lantern. I turn away, hear a key unlocking my cage while something hard is jabbed into my side. "Move back!" a guard aims the light. The door is relocked and the soldiers return upstairs.

When I open my eyes, rings of yellow and
white novas burn in front of me. I stare out, my
hands outstretched, unsure what has happened.
"Who's there?" I call.

The voice is not what I expect. "Mr. Mafante?"

Confused, I don't believe at first, am certain
I've misheard and will be attacked at any moment.
"Who is it?" I move further into the rear of my cell
where I crouch in the dark and hope to hide.

"It's me, Mr. Mafante. Over here," fingers
are snapped. "Mr. Mafante? Are you there?"

The voice is clearer now, unmistakable. I begin
moving toward the sound, reach for the click-click-
snapping, find Daniel's arm as he grabs my sleeve
and greets me with a sudden and mad embrace.

———

Leo Covings knew what he needed, up to a
point. He'd found his beginning, had his middle,
but not quite his end. To create the perfect final
scene, he require inspiration. Already bits of footage
had appeared in several countries on TV, the
ambush at the main warehouse mixing the perception
of news with a movie trailer tease. What fascinated
viewers was the hook, the promise of real events
unfolding in a feature Leo swore to finish soon.
This was the problem, how to complete what he
started, keeping everything real and not real, life
imitating art imitating life, the revolution that was
and wasn't his to shape in and away from the pre-
scripts of Teddy Lamb.

Katima had heard all the worst rumors about
the American director and assumed they were true.
"I suppose you must be wondering what I want,"
Leo passed the corporal who sat guest-like in the

kitchen, walked into the front room where Katima was drafting letters. He came to see her, he said, "Because you are now the tie that binds." He told her what André had wanted, how it was too soon to know which way things would turn out. "Despite a rough start." He spoke about his film, about Teddy and his movie. "My movie," Leo wanted her to understand. "What if I told you I don't know what's going to happen? And if I don't know, then Teddy can't."

He said he wanted her to help, that "This is why I'm here, to work with you on the end." He stood staring through his hands, framing Katima's features while he described the process for creating a final scene. "It's like adding bees and snakes to a jar and letting nature take its course. I want to see what happens once we put the pieces in place." Leo moved closer, could tell he had her attention, however much she wasn't sure that she could trust him. He came from the shadows, said "Listen, listen," was eager to discuss an idea he had.

———

A few days after Nick and Anita arrived, two more men came to the house and disappeared with Kart and Tobias upstairs. When the four of them left a short while later, Nick asked and was told only, "It's boys night out."

Dinner was a mix of brown rice and beans. Nick ate with Anita in the kitchen. Since their arrival, Kart kept them busy with minor errands and chores around the house. Nick asked questions, looked for clues of things to come but mostly Kart kept him in the dark. Upstairs later, he sat on the mattress with his back against the wall and removed his boots. "It isn't that I don't like him," he said of Kart. "It's just that I know his type."

"What type?" Anita dropped down on the opposite side of the mattress while Nick tugged off his socks and stretched his toes. "He's predictable, is all. What's the Warren Zevon song?" he decided on this as a point of reference. "He's just an excitable boy. He's like those graduate students back in the States who are always ready to protest something without really knowing what's going on."

"But this isn't the States."

"Right. That's what I'm saying. There's no such thing as a harmless rant here. All pseudo-revolutionaries become the real deal."

Anita folded her legs in and pulled off her shoes. "At least Kart's trying to do something."

"What's he doing? I mean really?" Nick slipped off his pants, stretched his left leg until his bare toes touched Anita's knee, testing her mood, relieved when she didn't jerk away. The one window in the bedroom was covered by a tan cotton curtain, the breeze shifting the material forward and back. "Its easy to get caught up in things," he said. "But you can't confuse effort for progress. We need to be sure what's going on is not just a lot of loud noise."

"Is that what you think this is?"

"I don't know. What does Kart tell you?"

"When?"

"When he talks to you."

"He doesn't tell me anything," Anita reached for Nick's foot and squeezed his arch. "He asks what I want. He says there are things I can do."

"What things?"

"To help," she pushed Nick's foot off and climbed to her knees, stood to undress. Nick wrapped his fingers around her ankle. After so many days he still hoped Anita would change her mind and agree to speak with Dukette but this hadn't happened. She was stubborn, impatient, entrenched. He looked toward their duffle, where the one book he brought with him, *Hern's Anthology of Modern Poetry*, was tossed. A gift from his mother, Nick was not initially a fan, but she convinced him Blake and Keats and Auden were the best companions when away from home, and he found in time this was true. He recalled parts of, 'O Tell Me the Truth about Love,' and "Does it howl like a hungry Alsatian/Or boom like a military band?" He thought of Auden's 'Lay Your Sleeping Head, My Love," and wished Anita would come back and settle down beside him.

"I just think it might be best," he mentioned again the American Consul, only Anita stopped him, annoyed. "If the Americans wanted to help my father they would have done so by now. If we go to him we're stuck. He'll want to know things we can't tell him."

"So instead we do what?" Nick wanted her to explain specifically so he could argue in turn, say that war gave license it was true, but to what end? "What about your father?" he tried again. "What would he say?"

"Nick, don't."

"I'm just asking."

"My father's in jail. That's where doing things his way got him. He trusted the wrong people and Teddy crushed him. I'm not going to do that. It's bad faith." This was her father's mistake, ignoring obvious truths. "It's false assumptions that let everyone down. Listen," she didn't want to fight anymore, came tired and lay beside Nick on the mattress. "Let's talk about it in the morning.

I know what you're saying. I do. We'll discuss it
tomorrow, I promise."

Nick slid closer along Anita's side. Tired,
he shut his eyes, told himself it was enough for the
moment, and soon fell asleep. In the dark, Anita
got up and went to the window where she waited for
what Kart said would happen. Just after 1:00 a.m.,
a blast lit the sky, loud and jarring, sending a sea
of colors soaring, followed immediately by the wail
of sirens and alarms. Nick woke startled. Anita
looked at him for a second before saying, "It's
alright. It's nothing," and turning away again to
face the flame, "Don't worry, go back to sleep."

———

———

I sit with Daniel against the bars, our feet
beneath the blanket as the rats are active. We hear
them scurry, shoo them off when they sniff too
close. I ask about my family, my father, Katima and
Ali, Emilo and the others, Bo and Cris and Feona,
but Daniel has nothing new. "I was hiding," he
tells me, and describes those first days following
the attack at the Port, how "They came for us, the
soldiers and police." A detention center was set
up at the Stadium, hundreds of people arrested, a
list posted and more names added by the hour. "I
managed to avoid them for almost a week but eventually they found me," Daniel said. "An American
soldier brought me in."

We sit for some time and talk. Everything
is dark. Finally a bit of sunlight passes across my
small window and I stare closer at Daniel. His black

hair is longer now, falls over the right side of his face. His cheeks are whiskered, his beard shorter than my own. I notice he has the usual bumps and scabs and bruises, though nothing of consequence, which comes as a great relief. I want to know more, all that has happened since his arrest, who has he seen at Moulane and what if anything has he heard? Instead of answering, he says, "Why, André?"

It's the first time I can recall his referring to me this way. His tone is wrenching and I think initially he's asking me to explain about the Port and why things went the way they did. I begin to apologize, my guilt in need of forgiveness, I say, "You're right. I should have thought things through more clearly. Daniel, I'm sorry." But he isn't listening, is asking instead, "Why have they brought me down here?"

I think at once of the Captain's threat, just as the door at the top of the stairs opens again and three soldiers come down. The light they carry is not as bright as before. I can see them enter my cell. The first guard pushes me aside, shouts at Daniel, "Visit's over." They grab his arms, re-lock my cage and disappear upstairs.

Hours pass. I wait for what I'm not sure, listen to every sound coming from above. At one point two new guards bring me water and a bowl of greenish-brown corn meal. I look for Daniel, ask nervously if they know where he is. The guards caw back at me, flap their arms like foolish birds, cup their hands to their ears and laugh, "Who? Who?" More time passes. Alone again, the waiting itself becomes a form of torture. Late that night a fresh light is shined down the stairs. I shield my eyes as two more guards approach my cell and shove Daniel back in on top of me. We both tumble as the door is relocked. The guards vanish, leaving the lantern behind.

Daniel stands in the half-light, his hands cupped against his middle, his shoulders sloped as if some great force is pressing down. I move quickly toward him, say his name, ask several times, "Are you alright?"

He turns away, not answering at first, moves toward the bars, sinks against them with his legs extended and his arms still cradled in against his belly. The lantern allows me to see his face gone pale. I kneel in front of him and ask again, "What is it? What's happened?" Daniel repeats my question as if he, too, is trying to make sense of it. "What exactly?" and unfolding his arms, he shows me the knife.

———

Katima agreed to wear the costume Leo gave her. At the south end of the University, she walked down the center of the grassy common, past Bolano Hall and the graduate library. Leo filmed her alone at first, framed against the sunrise. He used his own old Keystone Bel Air camera. Later, when more people came, he planned to have his crew shoot the scene with state-of-the-art equipment, but for now he wanted simply to get a sense of what was there.

"What I have is this," he pulled several pages of notes from his back pocket, a series of half finished dialogues, things to get people started. He explained how the end of his film had to resonate with the sort of integrity and spontaneity he couldn't predict, and asked Katima, "Tell me, what do you imagine?"

Teddy had his own idea for the final scene. "Picture this," he sent for Leo, cupped the American's elbow. Dressed in combat gear, with stars and boots and pistol polished to such a shine the light as he walked sparkled off his stride, he said, "What I want is a battle on the beach. I'll lead the charge, like Rommel in the desert. As fierce as Patton. As inspired as Washington crossing the Delaware, by George!" Outside the capital, the fighting had continued for weeks, drawing closer again back to the city. Teddy unhinged, put his faith in the magic of movies, insisted the finale be a spectacle. "If we get it on film, us winning the war, that will be that. There will be no disputing. The last scene should be of us returning, having smashed the rebels, the streets lined with people singing and dancing and cheering wild."

A movie scene, for sure. Leo said he could create the visuals no problem, "But this isn't what our film's about. John Wayne and Audie Murphy, Randolph Scott and Gary Cooper, Tom Hanks looking for Private Ryan. It's all been done a thousand times and what's the point?"

"The point is in Bamerita now I am John Wayne," Teddy waved his pistol which may or may not have been a prop. "If it's something real you want, we'll do it. We'll set the stage and make it happen. All we have to do is get the rebels to the water."

"This Teddy thinks," Leo told Katima, shook his head at the suggestion. "What sort of movie?" he frowned again. "What revolution ever ends so neatly? Even as a fiction, this is a bad one." He explained his plan once more, said to Katima, "I'll set the scene and let you make the ending happen."

Katima in the clothes Leo selected, a pastel sundress, cotton material, silver and gold hugging her hips, crossed the center of the common where she stopped and waited. She agreed to do as Leo asked even though she didn't yet completely trust him. There seemed something unsettled about his proposal, which he said was exactly the point. Still, "How is this any different?" she thought of the rally, of all that had happened before when they marched right into an ambush.

Leo perched high atop a painter's ladder, answered Katima's question with, "It's different because this time we're shooting blind." He regretted his word choice but smiled just the same, and seeing the first of the others arrive, both civilians and soldiers as word spread, he raised his camera and called for, "Action!"

——

Daniel cradles the knife in his hands, holds it there as I say his name, ask "What is this?" and wait until he answers. As soon as I understand, I turn and vomit what little food there is in my stomach, spit and cough up mostly acids and bits of old corn. "It's ok," I hear myself say, my voice strained, detached as if someone else is speaking. I move back and say again, "Ok. Don't worry." I find Daniel's eyes in the light of the lantern. Both of us by then are shaking, though as Daniel raises his arm to pitch the blade away, I catch his wrist, surprise myself by urging, "You have to."

"No."

"If you don't."

"It doesn't matter."

"But if you do, they've promised to let you go, didn't they?" It takes all my strength to continue, my encouragement not brave, a reflex I don't know for certain where it comes from. Daniel rocks forward and again covers the blade of the knife with his arms. How clever the Captain is, I think, assigning the task this way, orchestrating what seems a betrayal from within, making everyone believe the movement against Teddy is splintered and crumbling. "Don't worry," I try not to think. "The Captain will let you go. He wants you on the street. None of this does him any good if they don't release you. Once it's over," I tell Daniel, "as soon as you're out, you need to go to my father and let him know what's happened. He'll protect you from anyone who doesn't understand." My suggestion comes as yet another surprise, all of it swathed in a curious logic as I make clear, "My father's the only one who can defend you."

Everything now is madness. I imagine the Captain above delighted, how easily he's managed to arrange all this. Daniel goes and leans against the bars. The knife dangles loose in his grip. I stare at the edge, petrified by the prospect but force myself to ask, "How long?"

"Soon. An hour."

"Let me." I can't quite wrap my mind around the idea that any of this is real, and yet here we are. I wonder what others would do, Alina Pienkowska, Emilo, Georges Danton and Thomas Paine? What of my father and Gandhi? I want to say something to give us both courage, but all I can focus on is the feeling that I'm again about to vomit. "You'll need me to," I repeat my proposition, everything still a horror. If I was a braver man I'd have already stolen the knife, or bashed my skull against the wall, saving Daniel the trouble. But I'm slow and can't quite manage. "Let me," I offer meekly and don't extend my hand.

Daniel moves nearer the bars while I stand in the center of my cell, shaking worse than ever. "Here. Give me," I suggest again, hoping to find courage. "If you can do this," I say, "in a little while you'll be free."

The light from the lantern slips past me, casting Daniel inside a soft golden weave. I see his trembling slow then stop altogether, his eyes clear as he stares at me. I wait for him to say something but he's quiet now. (Gandhi said: "It is my unalterable conviction that even though the Government may not feel embarrassed in any way whatsoever by the incarceration or even execution of an innocent person... such incarceration and execution will be the end of that Government.") Only as I realize what Daniel's thinking do I scream, "No!" ("I do not wish to die," Gandhi said, "but I would welcome it... and love above all, to fade out doing my duty with my last breath.") The line of Daniel's jaw is set as he tips his head back, the full of his neck exposed, his throat stretched and arm extended as he groans twice, "Oh shit. Oh shit," before the blade passes into the light, crosses over and through, in and out, in and out, again and again and again.

CHAPTER 12

K art had Nick drive with Maria down into the underground lot of the hospital, where a man in a faded Cheap Tricks t-shirt and blue orderly slacks loaded the trunk with boxes. Ten minutes later, they headed out again across Kefuntin Boulevard. Before leaving the house, Nick had tried talking with Anita, but she bobbed and weaved beneath all attempts at conversation. "About last night," Nick had asked the others. Avene Delu in the kitchen opened an old can of tuna, soaked half a piece of toast in the oil, while Kart joked, "A bit of thunder is all. It's natural this time of year. Storms don't scare you, do they, Captain America?"

Anita slipped into the basement as Kart handed Nick a list. "Maria knows the way. Don't sweat the details. You're just along for the heavy lifting."

The roads on the west end of the capital were less patrolled, the houses and storefronts quiet. Maria told Nick where to turn. She hummed a song by James Taylor, 'Fire and Rain.' "Someone should write a song about all this, you know? I think everything important should be put to music."

A soldier's jeep ran a red light and disappeared behind a boarded over Cash 'N Carry. Maria pointed and told Nick, "Here." At the corner a series of shops gave way to houses on winding streets, wriggling worm-like closer to the bluffs and then the sands before the sea. Maria read the numbers, told Nick to "Slow down." The next two hours were spent delivering messages and boxes of supplies to addresses Maria had on a separate list. Twice Nick called Anita on the cell he had with him and twice she didn't answer. He checked his watch, was anxious to get back, an odd feeling in his gut. He was about to ask Maria how many more stops when she said, "Wait. Back up." Nick shifted into reverse, looked in the rearview mirror, parked and watched as the door opened and Paul Bernarr helped Justin Avere into the car.

—

By the time I grab Daniel's arm he's already starting to fall. My face, hands and chest are quickly wet, Daniel's throat parting like the fleshy seam of a cushion torn. He appears surprised by the sharpness of the blade, how easily it passes through, striking bone just below his jaw, the arteries clipped strings in a child's toy guitar. I put my hands on his shoulders, my head in his chest and push him back, only his legs buckle and he folds against me.

We crumble together, Daniel half in my lap. I cradle him much as I would an infant napping. His face is white, his eyes open, his mouth parted as if to speak. I rub his cheek, say "Daniel, Daniel, Daniel, Daniel." When I howl, the sound I make is loud and feral. I move us against the wall, sit there, Daniel's hands folded, his shoulders braced so his head and neck are supported before I crawl across the floor and wail louder. On my back, I lay in the center of my cell and stare up at the ceiling. My chest heaves against the sound of the guards moving above me in heavy boots. I'm sure they've heard my screams, and refusing them the satisfaction, I force myself to stop crying, relax my arms and slow my breathing down to nothing.

This is what I'm thinking when the door at the top of the stairs opens and I close my eyes, deny the guards any sort of reaction. Covered in Daniel's blood, I don't move at all, wait for them to stomp and kick me, and how strange then when I hear them talking. "Well done, howling boy," they say to Daniel sitting in the corner. "For this you're sure to get a medal." They reach down, grab my hands and feet, lift me from the floor and take me up the stairs where I'm brought into the yard outside, left beneath the now pale moon, laid out in the dirt of the rotted garden beside three other corpses to await the Captain's inspection.

—

Anita carried her bag into the hall. Near the stairs she retied her boots, glanced at the time, thought about Nick and hoped he was safe. She debated falsely the idea of staying behind, wondered if sneaking off would only make things worse. Yesterday Kart said, "If you're up for it. Maybe it's too much. Your American might mind. And your dad, if he was here." He left her for a

few hours and then came back. "This is it. It's
what there is. It's not so neat and tidy, this war,"
and leaning in as if to share a secret, whispered
"Shit, Anita. Shit, what did you come back for?"

Outside, Tobias brought a different car
around while Avene and Verne put the supplies
in the trunk. Kart sat up front, navigated as
they drove west, circled the capital, avoiding
checkpoints by cutting down side streets, crossing the Avenues when necessary, finally entering
Rosan Parks where the houses were large and
built up on a series of hills. Tobias slid the car
by lampposts, ducked and dodged the pockets of
light. When they reached Cheneslo Court, the
car lights were turned off. They drove a quarter
mile up and parked.

Kart got out and unlocked the trunk. At the
top of the hill, across a long stretch of lawn, was a
large house with wood panels and bay windows, a
roof that sloped down like an oversized hat and a
deck which extended around the entire left side of
the second level. The floodlights were on, sending
chalky beams of white far out across the yard. "No
guards," Kart handed one sack each to Verne and
Anita, keeping the third for himself. "After midnight
they all go inside and sleep like dogs."

Anita was assigned the far left wall, Verne
the right and Kart around back. Each timer was
set for six minutes. Tobias and Avene gave cover
while the others ran ahead, made their approach
low against the lights. Verne and Kart disappeared
around the rear of the house as Anita came in under
the deck, her pack set beside the gas line as instructed. "Here I am," she thought, "planting a
bomb." ("Here I am planting a bomb.") She expected to feel different, found nothing was as she

imagined, her adrenaline pitched and pumping, she seemed to be experiencing everything at a hundred miles an hour. "This is it," she thought of Nick. "This is real. This is all there is," and turning then she started running from the house back to the car. Pleased by her effort and the hard choices she was able to make, she got as far as the end of the patio before stopping suddenly, noticing as she hadn't before two children's toys there inside a small red wagon.

Verne was already racing toward the car, sprinting across the hill with Kart also dashing. "Fuck!" Anita moved quickly toward the bomb she set, cursed Kart again, and herself, unsure there was time to get all three packs and toss them clear of the house. Before she could decide, a light came on inside and Everett Doyle's sleep drawn face appeared on the opposite side of the sliding glass door. In pajamas and barefoot, his pot belly like a koala pushing through the gap in his pajama top, Doyle squinted and slid the door open, raised the pistol in his hand as Anita shouted, "Get out! Get out! Get the children out now!"

The floodlights found and lost Anita as she ran, the pop-pop-pop bringing Tobias and Avene further up the hill. A dozen rifle shots dropped Doyle in the grass, Anita screaming, clawing and cursing Kart from the back seat as everyone jumped into the car, the hillside going up in a succession of three loud blasts, the sky bright, bright, bright against the surrounding dark.

———

When I open my eyes there are stars, the sky overhead a sea of black on which a billion lights are floating. Slowly, I turn my head, manage to get my bearings and determine where I am in the yard. The bodies beside me are pale and dead, their faces filled with surprise. I roll on my side, move to my knees, then gradually to my feet. The prison's main floor is lit although the yard itself is dark. I consider for a moment rushing inside and shouting again "NBDF! NBDF!" letting everyone know I'm alive and that whatever they hear otherwise is a lie, but I can't quite bring myself to move toward the prison. The distance to the nearest wall is thirty yards, the height at nine feet too much for me to climb. I think of Daniel and wonder how long before the guards discover what has happened. Frightened, I race to the wall and leap straight up, my arms extending overhead, my body weak, stiff and bruised, I get no more than a few inches in the air, fail and fail and fail again to reach the top.

The ground beneath me is dry and brown, worn down long ago, with limited patches of weed and grass. What rocks there are remain half buried. I run from one to the next, scratching at the earth with my nails, trying to dig something free. I think if I can move just one, I'll be able to climb on top and scale the wall, but the rocks are too deep and heavy. I look toward the door, certain the Captain will come any second and shoot me, and terrified, I rush back across the yard, grab the first dead man by his hands and pull him to the wall. The man is large and gives me trouble. I bend him over until he's kneeling with his head in the ground, his hips pushed forward and shoulders drawn back as if in prayer. The second man is more my size and easier to haul. I find the waist of his pants, turn him over and hoist him up onto the big man's back. The third man is really just a boy, his arms tied behind him, his belly distended with something ruptured inside, his coloring more yellow than pale. I push him quickly onto the second man, lift him as best I can and climb on top.

The pile sags beneath me. I place my foot on the dead boy's head and launch myself up the best I can. The bodies give way a half-second after my fingers catch the top of the wall and I hang there, unable to move. The fear of dropping back into the yard is now a panic, and pulling harder, I lift enough to get a wrist and finally one leg over, flip and drop into the woods, tumble and roll and begin to run. The ocean is a mile to the north, Unamuno Boulevard above the shore winding west to the capital. I know I must avoid the roads as much as possible, plan to cover the three miles while it's still dark, and hope with luck not be caught before I reach the city.

———

Nick helped Dr. Bernarr bring Justin into the house. There in the front room, Justin spoke in whispers, his lungs inelastic, each word pried as thorns from his chest. His hair had turned completely white, his features faded, the edge to his cheeks and jaw worn back. "You are with Anita?" he asked and coughed, adjusted the tube beneath his nose, the hose extending from a small tank of oxygen Dr. Bernarr had started for him.

"The Mafantes are old friends," Paul Bernarr said. "André and Anita."

"And Ali," Justin looked toward Dr. Bernarr who brought his hands together in front of his chin. "About Ali then, yes." Later Dr. Bernarr took Nick aside and explained more. "This is the situation." A small machine was plugged into the wall, producing a medicated vapor which Justin breathed through a pale green mask. He told Nick where Kart and the others had gone. Nick stood by the window, listened to what Justin said about Everett Doyle. "A game of chess. Before we can get to the king, we have to work through pawns and bishops and rooks." He coughed, rubbed his throat, caught his breath and sipped from the water Maria brought him. "One piece at a time," he spoke of future plans and necessary efforts.

Nick wasn't listening anymore, was thinking about Anita. He excused himself, left the others in the front room and went upstairs where he emptied his duffle of everything but his camera. Carrying the duffle and camera back down, he slipped through the kitchen into the basement. The sticks of explosives were stacked on the shelves. Nick took what seemed like enough, along with an alarm already wired, a tube of epoxy and a metal box. He zipped his duffle and returned upstairs. In the front room he told the others he was going for a smoke, waited a minute then went out the back door, the car keys still in his pocket. He drove up the block, parked and waited.

Twenty minutes later Anita and the others returned. He saw Anita's arms rising and falling, flailing as she came from the curb and disappeared into the house. Relieved she was safe, not otherwise sure what had happened, Nick drove off.

Once inside Anita looked for Nick, finding instead Justin and Dr. Bernarr in the front room. Kart went directly to Justin who'd finished breathing the steam from the medicated inhaler and was again using the oxygen from the tank. Dr. Bernarr came from the old green chair and extended his arms, kissed Anita's cheeks.

The gravity of Justin's illness caught Anita by surprise, though rather than ask first about his health she pointed at Kart, shouting once more about Doyle until Justin intervened. "No decisions are made on their own."

"You?"

"Me."

"And the children?"

For a moment no one spoke. Kart shifted awkwardly. Dr. Bernarr listened from the chair, his head down, Verne and Avene by the archway, Maria near the hallway. The hum of air flowing from the tank was the only sound until Justin shut down the dial, removed the tube from beneath his nose and had Anita, "Come, sit by me."

Halfway downtown, Nick tried to remember the roads he and Maria drove earlier in order to avoid checkpoints. "A game of chess," he turned east, brought the car across Forbushe Avenue, recalled Robert Bye's poem, 'The Teeth Mother Naked At Last,' and 'Dedication,' by Czeslaw Milosz whose last stanza had always haunted him: "They used to pour millets on graves or poppy seeds/To feed the dead who would come disguised as birds./I put this book here for you, who once lived/So that you should visit us no more."

Just after 2:00 a.m., he turned down an alley, close enough to where he had to go in the morning. He shut off the car and cracked the window, made sure his duffle was alright then slipped into the back to catch a few hours sleep. He tried not to think too much about tomorrow, thought instead of the old Led Zeppelin song, "The Battle of Evermore," in which Robert Plant sang: "The pain of war cannot exceed/the woe of aftermath." He closed his eyes, pictured Anita, tried to imagine the tune as a love song. Instead, he remembered Ashbery's poem, "Girls On The Run and Dream Sequence." "The thread ended up on the floor/where all threads go./It became a permanent thing, like/silver:/ Every time you polish it, a little/goes away." He fell asleep then with no more poems in his head, the words as clouds waiting for him as he woke in the morning.

—

Gabriel Mafante sat behind the desk in his den, a small electric fan on the floor, the back door and windows boarded over by soldiers assigned to his arrest. The air in the house was a sticky soup, all personal effects, books and files and computer, television and radio, the couch and lowboy and standing lamp removed. Soldiers had also carried off the dining room table and tea service, silverware, maple sideboard and cabinet, the pictures from the walls and pillows from the bed loaded into a green government truck and driven away shortly after the ambush at the Port.

Here was the hoary core, Gabriel Mafante's existence redacted, he spent his days drafting a narrative exposing Bamerita's arthritic hips and knee joints. The discipline created a sense of routine, his confinement interrupted only in the evening as the Chief Inspector came to talk. Dressed as always in a rumpled white suit and heavy black shoes, Warez walked past the guard at the front door, sat on the one wooden chair left over from the dining room, removed his hat and asked, "Did you get out today? They're supposed to let you sit on the porch. Would you like to get some air?"

Gabriel Mafante kept his head down and continued to write. "Look," the Chief Inspector held up the bottle he'd brought, tried to sound cheerful, the way old friends will during a casual visit. "Let's have a drink. Let's not be sour."

"Is there news?"

"Nothing to speak of," the Chief Inspector rolled his shoulders, his usual poise replaced by tics and stutters. He patted his pockets for a cigarette then quickly got up. "Glasses," he disappeared into the kitchen, returned with two cups which he placed on Gabriel's desk. "Canadian V.O., not easy to come by. Here," he handed a glass to Gabriel who ignored the gesture and asked instead about André.

"No more than yesterday."

"Ali then?"

"The same."

"Katima?"

"She's fine. She's looked after." The list of people asked about since the start of the war was long, Davi Suntu, Don Pendar, Mical Delmont, Ryle Naceme among others, all bad news delivered with whiskey, sometimes sweet potatoes and canned meats. "Emilo Debor," the Chief Inspector two weeks ago had let his voice trail off.

Gabriel pushed his papers aside, got up from behind his desk, and carrying his whiskey walked on tired legs toward the kitchen. What food he had - rice and cheese, fruits and meat - the soldiers dipped into regularly, leaving him with but a few bags of grain, some vegetables and crumbs of angle food cake. "About all this," the Chief Inspector stood in the space where the breakfast table had been before the soldiers carted it away. As always, he tried to explain, feeling for some time the need, a regret he didn't quite know how to let go of. "If I could," Warez said, while Gabriel answered without expectation, his reply a summons in the form of a question, "What, Franco?"

Half drunk already, the Chief Inspector raised his glass, shook his head, started again, then stopped. Gabriel Mafante at the kitchen counter, began cutting up what vegetables he had on hand. "If you're hungry," he offered.

"No, no. That food is yours."

"As you've left me." The kitchen became quiet. A minute went by before the Chief Inspector said, "Yes, well, I'll let you have your dinner." He returned to the front room, bent down to pick up his hat, pulled the brim forward as if securing it against a high wind, and leaving the bottle on the desk, said "Good night."

He made three stops before heading home just after midnight. Casmola, he knew, would not be there. A week ago his wife said she was leaving to stay with relatives outside the capital where it was safe. An hour later, the officer assigned to the Bameritan Hyatt reported Casmola heading up to Leo's room. The Chief Inspector shrugged and unlocked his front door, entered the dark. He took off his coat and hat and shoulder harness and dropped them on the couch. In the bedroom he stripped off the rest of his clothes, went into the bathroom and rinsed his arms and neck, then sat on the edge of the tub and put his face in his hands.

The buzz in his head was heavy from whiskey. "About all this," he said as before, hoping to answer there in his own house. Unable still, he shrugged his shoulders, got up and slipped into bed, pulled the sheet around his middle and drifted off. His rest was intense, his dreams of recent history, the depth of his unconsciousness weighted like stones thrown down a well. He didn't stir for some time and woke only to the feel of something hard pressed against his cheek.

CHAPTER 13

n the woods I concentrate on not getting lost. I stay clear of the roads as long as I can, tracking my travels by the stars, north and east, while keeping an eye on the moon as I near the capital. The woods don't extend the entire way however, and there are gaps I must pass through, open areas where soldiers on patrol might easily spot me. Without shoes, I trot and stumble, enter the city and fold myself into the shadows. The thought of reaching my father's house, All Kings, or home to Katima tempts me, but these are places I'm sure to be looked for and so I shift my focus and head elsewhere.

My hair has grown out and becomes matted with sweat as I run. I try not to think too much but it's impossible. The door to the Chief Inspector's house is locked tight. I check the windows, test each pane of glass, tap a stone into the corners to see if one might crack. After several failed attempts I discover if I work the wood in one particular section

I can wedge out the surrounding frame. The process
takes nearly half an hour, before I can push enough
of the glass in to get my hand around. I wiggle the
single sheet free, reach in for the latch, lift the
window and climb inside.

My eyes are by this point well adjusted to
the dark, and passing the couch I spot what Warez
has left there. The hallway leads back to the main
bedroom where I hold the gun against the Chief
Inspector's cheek, say his name and turn on the
lamp. Warez squints, moves away from the gun.
He looks at me, uncertainly at first, takes in the
cuts and bruises, my soiled clothes, the stench
of my body, the weight shorn from my frame, my
beard and the dirt which clings to my flesh layer
after layer. The blood on my feet stains his floor.
"André?"

"Katima."

"She's alright. But how did you?"

"Ali? And my father?"

"Your father's fine. He's under house arrest. He's
a bull. He's well. Ali we haven't heard though,"
the Chief Inspector slides up and wraps the bed
sheet around his middle. "How did you get here?"

I hold the pistol out, the gun awkward in my
grip, my hand trembling as I ask about Emilo, Davi
and the others. My knees give and I struggle not
to shout, my free hand fisted in the air as I make
the Chief Inspector tell me about the Port.

"It's not what you think," Warez lifts his
chin, sits up and wraps the sheet tighter around
his stomach. His midsection is a pool of soft flesh.
I look quickly around, having forgotten and ask,
"Where's your wife?"

"She's not here. She won't be coming back.
Do you mind?" he motions toward his pants but I

wave the gun. The Chief Inspector lets his shoulders sag as if all of everything is a tremendous burden, and breathing deeply, he sits back down and repeats, "Things aren't what you think." He looks at my feet, suggests I bathe and tend to my wounds, proposes fresh clothes, a razor and something to eat, but I'm not interested in any of this and let him know, "That's not why I'm here."

"No, of course not," he shifts forward once more and begins to get up. I aim the gun at his heart but the Chief Inspector says only, "If you've come to kill me." He stands naked, "Otherwise, I'd like to get dressed."

I let him go to his bureau and pull on a fresh pair of undershorts and t-shirt. It occurs to me only after he opens his drawer that he might have a weapon inside, but by then it's too late. Warez turns and shows me the pistol before tossing it on the bed. "Come on," he grabs his pants, signals for me as he walks out of the bedroom.

I follow him through the front room where he examines the window. "Clever. Remind me to get that fixed." He proceeds to the kitchen, flips on the low light of the stove while instructing me to, "Sit. I'm going to fix you something to eat." He has fresh eggs in his refrigerator which he prepares in a pan scrambled with cheese. As he cooks, he keeps his back to me, speaks in a steady tone, repeats everything from the beginning, admits to telling Teddy about the Port. "I told him so he wouldn't do what he did. Do you understand? I felt if he knew your rally was harmless he wouldn't be surprised and send his soldiers in. I took a chance. I didn't think. The same as you," the Chief Inspector says this as a matter of fact, turns and glances at me, makes reference to my own mistakes, says "Hindsight's a whore, isn't she, André? She may seem to set the situation right, but in the end you're still fucked."

I sit at his table and say nothing. "I did not betray you," he insists. "I'd like you to believe this, but I can't make you. Still, just stop and consider, why would I, as Chief Inspector, want to start a war when I believed all you planned was a peaceful march?"

He talks more of Teddy, of Don Pendar, Emilo and Davi Suntu. For my friends I slump and weep. When I tell him about Daniel the Chief Inspector sighs, gives me time. He serves my eggs with salt and jam. Joining me, his face is a puzzle, a calm I can't quite make sense of, a weariness given way to something else. "I'm glad you're here," he says, confusing me further. The gun is on the table between us now. I've washed my hands so that my fingers are clean but the dark dirt is there still at the start of my wrists. I eat my eggs while the Chief Inspector taps the table near the gun, and referring once more to Teddy says, "Alright then, now that you're here, what are we going to do about all of this?"

———

Nick woke in the back seat of the car, the sunlight from the end of the alley rolling in through the rear window. The air was hot. He drove toward the center of the capital where soldiers stopped him twice at checkpoints and asked for ID. The camera and metal box loaded with explosives were underneath the front seat. The back of the car and trunk were searched but otherwise the soldiers didn't bother. Outside the American Embassy the streets were crowded. Wooden barricades stood

in orange rows, creating pockets of further separa-
tion. Nick parked and walked the last few blocks.
The first guard asked to see his papers, patted him
down, had him remove his shoes.

"Consul Dukette is expecting me," Nick tried
this. A second guard took his name, made him wait
just inside the Embassy doors while the guard at
the main desk used a black telephone to ring the
Consul's office. Two minutes later a woman in a
beige skirt, flat gold shoes and bone white blouse
came down and brought Nick upstairs. The halls of
the Embassy were long and shaded, the main lobby
without windows, everything cast dimly like the
inside of a cave. Nick had a yellow visitor's pass
hung from a thin chain around his neck. The soldiers
stationed on each floor watched as he walked by.

"Nick!" The Consul's office was on the third
floor where Eric Dukette was waiting. "Come in,
come in. I'd no idea." He removed a mound of files
from a flat cushioned chair. "When did you get
here?"

He took a seat, waited as Dukette pulled the
chair from behind his desk around in front and sat
beside him. "I'm on assignment," he said. "CAN."

"Ah, yes. Not vacationing then? Ha! But
things are locked down pretty tight. Someone
should have told me earlier. We're supposed to be
notified about people arriving. Not that we have
many these days. All the same, you should have
reported in, though I guess here you are," he
turned in his seat, reached and fumbled through a
stack of papers on his desk. "CAN you say?"

"That's right."

"Someone should have told me," he repeated
before giving up the hunt. "Ahh well, you're here now
and it's great to see you. When was the last time?"

"Portugal, three years ago."

"That's it. Your father and I were banging about at some conference and you came down. How is old Chuck?"

"He's good. He sends his best."

"And mine in turn. Tell him, will you?" On the wall to the right was a lithograph of Ted Williams in full swing, a map of the region pinned beneath, an umbrella stand across the way inside of which were three wooden walking sticks. A full length mirror was turned for some reason toward the wall, while a spare suit and shirt hung on a single wooden hanger behind the door. Dukette reached forward and squeezed Nick's knee. "It's good to see you," he said again. "Too few friendly faces of late. So, I take it you're here to cover our little tilt?"

"The revolution," Nick tried to sound convincing. "My bosses want to know why America's supporting Teddy."

"For the record?" Dukette lit a cigarette. "Off the record I'll tell you the General isn't a fellow one chooses to support. It's more complicated than that. The situation in Bamerita isn't like a sporting event where you pick a side, sit in the stands and cheer. Its a matter of greater interests. Bamerita presents us with certain strategical advantages, sitting where she does," Dukette emphasized. "For the moment Teddy provides a certain convenience. A bird in the hand," the American Consul found an ashtray on the floor and flicked the end of his cigarette into the bowl.

Nick nodded his head as if taking mental notes. "And the Port?"

"What of it?" Dukette blew smoke. "There's an ongoing investigation into that affair and that's

all I can tell you. How the war started, when it
started, at the Port or in the hills, who fired first,
he said, she said, none of it matters. Politics is
worse than business. At the end of the day its all
bottom line, who's scratching whose back and who
owes whom what."

Nick said, "I understand." He told Dukette,
"I'll keep that in mind," and asked again, "About
the General. I've a favor. I was hoping you'd help
me get a shot. Something exclusive."

"Were you now?" Dukette smiled at this.
"There are a good many people who'd like to get a
shot at Teddy."

"On film. I need something new. Some current
footage," Nick wiped his hands on the side of his
jeans. "If you could arrange this."

"You assume the General and I are close?"

"Off the record?" Nick tried a joke. "If
Teddy's scratching your back I figure you'll know
where to find him."

The American Consul laughed, considered
the request, weighed the possibilities, complimented
Nick on taking advantage of his connections. His
square face was creased by a series of deep sun
baked lines. He reached and slapped Nick's leg for
a final time, said "Well then, young Nick, if that's
all you're asking, let's see what might be done."

———

I eat my eggs, wipe clean every last trace
before going with the Chief Inspector back to the
bedroom. Of our plan we say nothing further, all of
it still but a rough outline, the equivalent of stage
directions. I make clear, "Before we go, I'd like to
see Katima first. And my father."

"We can do that," Warez has received phone calls this morning, has gotten word that Everett Doyle has been killed, informs his men that he's handling a different matter and tells me then, "No one's mentioned you as yet, André. I'm not surprised," he says. "Those at Moulane will want to keep things quiet for now. My guess is they'll order up a search on their own first, but word will get out soon and they'll have to make an official statement. Until then," he goes to his dresser and removes a fresh set of underclothes and socks. "A little big but they'll do. First, let's get you in the shower."

I've brought the gun from the kitchen, but toss it now beside the other on the bed. In the bathroom I turn on the tap, strip off my clothes and enter the flow. The warm water rinses me, the cuts on my arms and legs and feet sting, the bruises and bumps old and new still painful. The mix of dirt and blood and flakes of flesh swim down and disappear in the drain. Warez stands just outside the bathroom and tells me more about the revolution, all the news I didn't know. I come from the shower and dry myself with a towel, my body shrunk and bony. At the mirror I trim the whiskers from my face with a scissors, then wet the hairs again and apply shaving cream, drawing the sharp edge of the razor down my cheek. My hand shakes and twice I have to stop and collect myself, thinking of Daniel. I do not shave my head.

The Chief Inspector brings me a shot of whiskey which I sip in the hope of steadying my hand. When I finish in the bathroom, I begin to dress in the pale blue shirt and brown slacks Warez has provided. The pants are too big, but we make them work with a brown belt. The shirt fits better. The

Chief Inspector goes to his closet again and pulls out an old beige sports coat, holds it up for me, taking measure, saying "When I was a few years younger and a pound or two lighter."

It's now just after six in the morning. Exhausted, I have no interest in sleep, stand for a moment and try to compose myself. The Chief Inspector, too, seems anxious. He collects the guns from the bed, slips on his shoulder holster and hands the second pistol to me. In 1948, Gandhi wrote: "An eye for an eye makes the whole world blind." I don't want to think of this, believe it's best now if I don't think at all. In my run through the woods, I stopped at one point to catch my breath, and sitting on a rock, panting and sweating beneath the moon, I saw on the ground several hundred red harvester ants marching toward me. I looked closer, startled and unsure how they noticed me there, whether it was the fresh cuts on my feet or if by accident I'd stumbled into their nest. I moved my legs but the ants veered with me, proceeding in unison, determined to reach me until I bent down, and spotting the largest ant in the front of the pack, I crushed it dead. Instantly then the other ants scattered.

I place my feet in two soft pairs of socks and slip on the most flexible shoes the Chief Inspector can find. The ache in my arch, toes and heels causes me to think of Emilo and once more I'm overwhelmed. The Chief Inspector waits for me to finish sobbing, does not ask questions or suggest I sip more whiskey. Across town, my father is just settling in behind his desk when we arrive. He watches us approach from the far end of the hall, recognizes me at once and comes to meet my embrace. "Skin and bones," he says, and there's a tremble in his voice. He looks toward the Chief

Inspector who tips his hat and turns away. "How then, André?" he wants to know, pulling at the hairs on my head.

Warez has phoned ahead and told one of his men to bring Katima here. Soon after the Chief Inspector's cell rings and we learn Katima is not at home and the corporal assigned to watch her can't be located either. "It's no doubt nothing," Warez says, and asks me then if I prefer to wait, which I do, of course. I'm nearly delirious in my desire to see Katima, am tempted to go to the house myself but know this is not a good idea. I want to speak with her friends and clients, to drive through the city and howl her name, but instead I say, "If we haven't heard by noon we should leave."

"For where?" my father wants to know.

I create a story, pretend that Warez and I are to meet with officers in the army who wish to sever their alliance with Teddy. My father, of course, does not believe me. His eyes find mine and insist I return his stare. To the Chief Inspector he says, "So much talk all these nights, Franco, and here all you were missing was André."

We eat in the kitchen, my sore feet forcing me to sit on the stool while my father stands and prepares fruit slices and squares of bread. The Chief Inspector makes several more calls. We discuss separate arrangements for my father, make plans to move him somewhere safe but he refuses to go, says "I'll wait here for you to come and get me." Later, at the front door he touches the Chief Inspector's shoulder, draws me in and holds me close. His hands are mammoth paws still strong, he doesn't let go for the longest time. I leave then with the Chief Inspector and slide back inside the car.

CHAPTER 14

Teddy turned to Leo and said, "Explain it to me again. What exactly's supposed to happen?"

Back before the coup, Bamerita established a Natural Energy Center to reduce dependence on imported oil. The plan was to apply Jacques-Arsene d'Arsonval's theory for creating electricity by combining cool and warm ocean waters, producing steam to power turbines in a plant built on shore. Teddy abandoned Dupala's idea once he discovered the 2,000-foot deep seawater pipeline supplied a more immediately marketable product; desalinated water, tens of thousands of years old, absent pollutants and rich with traces of phosphorus and calcium. The water was pumped to the surface and bottled as, 'Bamatine, The World's Most Wholesome Beverage!'

Since the trailer for the unfinished Leo Covings' film first appeared overseas, sales for Bamatine more than tripled. People began looking for Bamerita on maps and Google searches. Several countries including the United States ran old episodes of *General Admission* on cable. The spark of celebrity brought Teddy windfalls he quickly exploited. Each day he checked the late night ratings of *General Admission*, calculated the most recent sales of Bamatine, spoke with his advisors about producing souvenirs, t-shirts and stickers for merchandising. The media took note, ignored at first the small matter of the revolution, concentrating instead on the fifteen minutes of fame afforded General Lamb.

Only after initial interest in Teddy died down did editors and producers decide to take a serious look at the war. Reports appeared claiming, "startling revelations," about what had happened at the Port. With Teddy's character under fire, 'General Admission' was pulled from the fall schedules. Sales of Bamatine declined then fell off altogether. "What do we do?" Teddy turned to Leo.

"Not to worry," Leo explained the three dramatic stages of rise, fall and resurrection. "The hero must take his lumps in the second act. Look at Travolta. Look at Polanski. Look at Richard Nixon for Christ's sake. You can't bully your way back. You have to let the audience believe you've earned redemption." He assured Teddy the scene at the University would provide him the opportunity. "All you have to do is show a little forbearance and give the audience something to embrace."

"But what is this scene?" Teddy still did not understand. "What's going to happen?"

"What indeed," Leo said no more than this, mentioned instead a separate scene he planned to shoot with Teddy and splice into the mix. "I promise you'll come off looking better than Gary Cooper in 'High Noon.' Better than Jimmy Stewart in 'Mr. Deeds.' You know the pictures? I'm thinking Oscar. You'll be hotter than hot then, you'll be electric."

———

Early the next morning, Katima stood in the center of campus, a few yards from where she spent the better part of the night. People here and there had wandered down, the cameras rolling in anticipation of some as yet unspecified event. Others watched the live feed on the screen in the Plaza before making their way to the University, while soldiers both sent and curious stood at the opposite end of the grassy common.

The corporal assigned to Katima sat off to the side, on a cement bench in front of the graduate library. Leo perched himself high above the lawn in one of those hydraulic cherry picker baskets. Katima looked at him but did not acknowledge his wave.

———

Out in front of the American Embassy, Nick passed between the wooden barricades, the piece of paper Dukette provided to show the General folded in his pocket. "No promises," the American Consul said he would try and arrange things, explained how Teddy spent less time in the capital these days. "For obvious reasons. Here," he rooted through his desk, gave Nick a cell phone, told him to, "Just sit tight until you hear from me."

In the car Nick read the note, turned on the phone, slid everything out from beneath the seat and arranged the explosives in the metal box. He fixed the camera on top to make the two separate pieces seem connected. The result was awkward and unlikely to fool anyone. "What now?" He put the box and camera into the leather bag he brought, the fit snug and almost convincing. Ten minutes later he was driving east out of the capital. He parked a few miles away, near a bluff past the woods overlooking the water. The sky was empyrean blue. He thought of the last time Anita and he made love, pictured her body ginger and soft, her thighs in their grip as she lifted and fell over him. How easily he let himself go then, and how much of everything now was inspired by his need to be there again.

The air inside the car was a pitch steam hot. Nick wiped his hands down the front of his shirt, ran through a list of how things were supposed to go. His plan was crudely formed, without specific details from this point on. He considered the next step, and then the whole of what he was doing, what sense it made and didn't make. He though of Anita once more, and when the phone rang at noon and the American Consul told him, "You're in," he hardened his focus and thought of nothing else.

Directions were given, instructions how to get across the highway. The drive took twenty minutes. Nick felt the breeze through the car window, breathed in the smell of the sea. The house was smaller than he expected, a cottage with a flat roof and white wooden siding, one of several shelters Teddy used as a dodge during the war. Nick stopped a hundred yards up and set the timer on the alarm, checked the minutes against his watch before putting everything back in the bag. A poem by Frances E. W. Harper came to him, "A Story of the Rebellion," which included the lines: 'Someone, our hero said/must die to get us out of this/ Then leaped upon the strand and bared/His bosom to the bullets' hiss.' He touched his chest above his heart and said, "What the fuck."

A second car was just arriving as Nick drove closer. A man in a rumpled white suit, black moustache and panama hat got out, followed by another more slender man wearing a poorly fitted suit and walking as if his shoes hurt his feet. The guards greeted the two men and let them pass up to the house. Nick, in turn, was stopped before he could get near the gate, the two soldiers running toward him, both in green uniforms, with brown boiled faces. They pointed at Nick with their rifles, motioned at his bag and told him to, "Put it down!"

In response, Nick waved the letter from Dukette, said "The General's expecting me. The American Consul called." He unzipped the leather bag, wanted them to see the camera on top, hoping that would be enough. "Here," he said. "Here," and continued to wave the letter. The nearest soldier grabbed the paper while the second snatched the bag, was about to inspect the contents when something from inside the house caused him to stop and run with the other guard through the front door.

—

I tell the Chief Inspector to move away from me. "There's no need, Franco," I say, but he answers, "We'll see." The soldiers recognize Warez and let us pass. We're greeted the same way as we enter the house, are escorted down a long hall toward Teddy's office where we find him standing behind a mahogany desk, a folder opened and held flat in his hands. There are two other men with him,

a priest and an American in uniform I don't recognize. Teddy glances up from the material he's
reading, his face dark, his features strained. He
looks nothing like a movie star, has on large black
framed glasses which he doesn't wear in public,
his hair brushed back and the jacket of his uniform unbuttoned. He greets the Chief Inspector,
acknowledges me, gives a curious stare, and then
the priest is pointing.

Gandhi said: "I object to violence because
when it appears to do good, the good is only tem-
porary; the evil it does is permanent." I thought
of this before, down in my cell where I also wondered, *But what of the evil that remains if you
don't kill it?* I fumble for my gun, stand without
illusion, completely resigned, knowing who I am
and what went wrong and why then can't I shoot?
I curse myself and still I'm unable to raise my
gun, am about to put it down when I see Teddy
reaching inside his jacket. The Chief Inspector
notices all and in an instant fires and hits his
mark. The priest jumps and shouts, then steps
aside as Teddy falls.

I turn toward the American colonel who's
also surprised and only now reaching for his pistol.
Reconciled, I wait to receive the counterblast while
giving the Chief Inspector time to run, but Warez
has his own plan and saves me again with a second
shot.

The sound of gunplay brings the soldiers
racing into the house. Warez shouts, drags me
with him. We dash back down the hall where the
Chief Inspector points for the guards, "In there!
In there!" confusing them for a moment as they
rush past. One of the soldiers is carrying a large
leather bag, I'm not sure why. Everything's a

blur. My head pounds, I find myself contrite and at the same time calm, if not at peace then near enough. Gandhi said: "I believe forgiveness is more manly than punishment... But forgiveness only when there is the power to punish... A mouse hardly forgives a cat when it allows itself to be torn to pieces." To this I've earned the right to forgive and be forgiven, I think, though even after all of this I can't be sure.

There's nothing now to do but run. Satyagrahi bids goodbye to fear but what of the rest? I think of Tamina, of Katima and my children in front of me, am wanting then when I'm lifted suddenly and sent flying over floors no longer there. The roof goes missing, the air now grey while I soar through a bright white patch of starlight. Everything disappears in a deep ivory flash, the entire house demolished, as if an enormous fist has ripped through the ground and sent us broken and burning into the sun.

———

That afternoon, the campus grew crowded as more people came. Leo stayed in his lift overhead, watching Katima and the others, waiting for something to complete his film. The area in the middle of the lawn remained vacant, a gap of some twenty yards dividing soldiers from the rest. Katima sat near the edge, her legs beneath her crossed. People gathered in small groups, whispered among themselves. The cameras ran, recorded the stillness. Two Port-A-Johns were sent for as Leo knew better than to risk blowing a scene because an actor had to take a crap.

Others outside gathered at the gate of the University, the sight of soldiers making them nervous.

Only the movie cameras and Leo's assurances assuaged their alarm. "Come on, come on," he called to those hovering on the periphery, "Don't be shy." Food was brought in shortly after noon, sandwiches and cupcakes Leo had delivered to the center of the lawn. At first people approached with caution, snatching a meal and moving back. The soldiers, too, seemed uncertain, bringing their rifles as they went for the food. Katima found the corporal still sitting on the cement bench, brought him a turkey sandwich and a quarter bag of chips. After this everyone realized there was enough to share and took just what they needed.

They sat among themselves and ate, each on their side of the lawn. Drawn to the food, bees buzzed, one yellow jacket invading the loose fit of a woman's blouse. As she jumped and threw her hands and legs in the air, Leo took the initiative, signalled at once for music. The sound engineer pressed on R.E.M.'s *Losing My Religion*. Seeing the woman, others got up to dance. The soldiers as well, happy after their meal, having set down their rifles and looking for something to do, came toward the song.

The wind changed. The day went from warm to hot as the air stirred in from the sea. The waters rose and rolled beneath the island. Floating free all these many thousands of years, Bamerita's movement, inch by inch, east and south, was subtle even in the fiercest storms. Sometime shortly after 1:00 p.m. however, the ground began to rumble. Perhaps it was the dancing, or the game of frisbee which broke out with soldiers and people tossing back and forth their sandwich plates. Maybe it was the plates themselves, set deep in the tuff and soil, laid like ancient china resting on buried shelves sliding across the substratum by way of palaeomagnetic ticks. Or it may have been the latest blast which occurred outside the capital and shook things up all on its own.

When word first reached the University about Teddy, traveling as always with the alacrity of birds, people waited for confirmation, and when that came just as quickly all the dancing stopped. Games of toss and tag and casual mingling ended, the soldiers separating one by one from the people. The music that was playing - *Beautiful Day* by U2 - was turned off, the sides dividing as if the tremble in the ground below had shaken them apart. The roar of thunder rose, a clap before the first shower of rain. Katima saw the soldiers move for their rifles and people slipping off again quite nervous.

She thought of Medha Patkar then, the disciple of Gandhi she'd read of in one of André's books. The legend of Medha had her trying to drown herself in protest against the government-built Sardar Sarovar dam which ruined the fishing in the Narmada River and forced the resettlement of more than 200,000 indigenous people in India. In 1999 Medha stood in frigid monsoon waters for 30 hours, waiting for the rains to bring the river over her head, only to be pulled out in the last moment by soldiers sent to keep her from becoming a martyr. Katima looked overhead, up into the rain. She thought of Medha drowning, and not drowning, thought of André, not yet knowing, wondered about tomorrow and tomorrow and where would she go if she left now?

She went to sit in the center of the lawn.

Others turned and saw her. A young woman Katima didn't recognize though she looked somehow familiar, came in from the gates, having walked

from the house where she was staying, sat then as
well, there in front of the soldiers. In the space
between, another man and then two women more
came to sit. A corporeal across the way sat, followed
by two others. A man who noticed Katima called
her by name and also sat down, and then more of
the soldiers. The rain fell, and steady, too; people
sat and the soldiers each in their turn. Everyone
faced one another, silent and still, as if in worship,
for the longest time.

Nothing happened after that.

This is what Leo Covings filmed.

CHAPTER 15

"Lucky you weren't there," the American Consul said to Nick about the blast. "A few minutes earlier and you'd have been worm chum as well."

More American soldiers arrived that week. "To keep the peace," Dukette explained. A list was compiled of would-be candidates to take over the presidency, with Gabriel Mafante the popular choice. Open elections were promised eventually, though a counsel of American and Bameritan businessmen, ex-senators and old soldiers was assembled to review the situation and run the country, Dukette said, "For now."

"You see?" Kart let the others know. "All of everything and for what?" He thought of Kara and Angeline, of days in waters warm and nights when nothing was impossible. The following afternoon he drove to All Kings where 200 American troops were quartered. He slowed the car, leaned out the open window and threw something over the fence.

The night after burying her father, Anita sat up late with Nick. Word of André came in the aftershock, the Chief Inspector said to have brought him across town as a recaptured prize for Teddy when the building blew. (Other stories told were dismissed by the press as too fantastic.) "I can't believe," Anita went three days earlier with Feona into the woods, and knelt where Ali was buried, there among the last of the children. Markers were set stone upon stone, piles of rocks in a patch of forest near the first hill where grass and weed would eventually grow over. Together they piled flint and rock, said the names of all those shorn as flowers wild and cut with long blades sharp and glinting. Feona held the final stone to place atop Ali's marker, the one with the pointed edge used to carve his name into the ground.

Anita leaned her chin against Nick's arm. "I'm going to stay. Can you stay?"

He touched her hair, slid his fingers down to the smooth warmth of her neck. The blast produced was much stronger than he expected, the roar and flames and pieces of sky raining down as he dove for cover. He lay in bed that night beside Anita, picturing again the man walking with shoes that hurt his feet. In disbelief, he remembered the poem, 'Celebration:' "At night/boys pick house sparrows/from traps; tie tiny/bombs to bird-packs/and let the sparrows go/ free, black silhouettes/against the haze of stars./The bombs explode in/swirls of burning feathers./The boys celebrate Independence./ Wings fly apart."

Nick reached for Anita's hands, found her fingers and tangled them around his own. "I'd like," he said. "I want to stay. If you want me to," and then he told her.

Katima in the backyard, brought with her planks of wood, nails and glue and tools. She carted up the wood and seaweed used at the cliffs as well, back when André was still in prison. The foundation was set from within, weighted by sand and blocks of cinder. The first pieces attached were photographs of André, and later Ali. The articles which followed were of Bamerita, and then as the tower grew, she attached all the other stories that moved her.

The sky turned blue as sapphire, smooth with brush strokes of white for clouds. Katima had a bottle of wine and sipped as she worked. Yesterday she saw the latest rushes of Leo Covings' film, the American having shown her first as promised. The movie surprised her, the context and composition honest. Leo laughed as she told him this. "What did you expect?" He didn't mention the rumors, reports of peculiar fragments in Teddy's skull. As things were now, there seemed no reason.

Leo came again that afternoon to say goodbye. In the backyard, he placed his hand against the wood of the new tower. Katima felt the ground beneath her soft from the rains, all the rolling on the waters having slowed again. The shifting was tenuous, and once more routine, as Bamerita drifted by degrees. Katima looked at the photograph of André as shot a few weeks before the War of the Cameras. She ran her hand across his cheek, wondered then as she had for days and resigned herself to never knowing.

All of this she thought again just as the blast at All Kings brought sirens and soldiers back into the street and four jeeps chased Kart as he drove away. There came in rapid succession more gunfire and sirens and another bomb exploding. Leo walking to his car, heard the blast as well and laughed. "Listen to that," he cupped his ears. "I haven't even released our film and already people are crying for a sequel."

——
——

ACKNOWLEDGMENTS

To the usual gang of suspects, my heartiest of thanks for their support: my friends and family at Dzanc Books and Black Lawrence Press, my partner and twin-son-of-a-different-mother Dan Wickett, the inimitable and sage guru Steven Seighman, my great editors and colleagues Diane Goettel and Colleen Ryor. To Keith Taylor for lending me a quote and being always the patron saint. To Laura Snyder and Jeff Parker for faith. To my mom and brother, always, and to dad still watching. To my wife, Mary, and kids, Anna and Zach, thanks guys, truly. Without you, none of this matters.